GR

SANDRA BROWN

LOVE'S ENCORE

WARNER BOOKS

A Time Warner Company

To Michael—
You are the sunshine of my life. . . .

Cover design by Jackie Merri Meyer
Cover photo by Herman Estevez

This Warner Books Edition is published by arrangement
with the author.

Warner Books, Inc.
1271 Avenue of the Americas
New York, NY 10020

W A Time Warner Company

Printed in the United States of America

BOOKS BY SANDRA BROWN

Another Dawn
Best Kept Secrets
Breath of Scandal
Charade
Eloquent Silence
Exclusive
French Silk
Hidden Fires
Mirror Image
Shadows of Yesterday
The Silken Web
Slow Heat in Heaven
Sunset Embrace
A Treasure Worth Seeking
Where There's Smoke
The Witness

One

*C*amille brought her compact car to an abrupt stop as she caught her first glimpse of Bridal Wreath. She had followed the directions given her at the tourist information office in historic Stanton Hall and taken Homochitto Street from downtown Natchez. The lady behind the desk told her that the lane leading to the old mansion would be on her left just before the road she was on intersected with Highway 65.

She almost missed the small, weather-faded sign obscured by thick shrubbery designating that this unpaved trail was the driveway she sought. She wended her way over the deep potholes while marveling at the enormous oaks trailing their gray, beardlike moss from branches of inestimable proportions; the magnolias that still retained a few creamy, fragrant, white blossoms, despite the lateness of the season; and the fountainlike formation of the shrubs lining the drive that had given the plantation house its name. The snowy flowers of the bridal wreath had long since disappeared in the summer's heat, but the branches were thick with their dainty, bright green foliage.

Camille opened the car door and stepped out, leaving the engine to idle. She gazed at the house before her. The basic facts of its history flashed through her mind. It had been built in 1805. The colonial architecture depicted the period. It had two stories. The rooms on the second floor opened onto a balcony that provided a roof for the front porch surrounding the first floor on three sides. The structure was red brick, though the years had faded the color to a dull rose. Six white columns rose majestically from the porch to support the balcony. Tall, wide windows flanked by forest green shutters were symmetrically spaced, three on each side of the huge front door, which was white. Suspended on a heavy chain was a brass chandelier hanging just over the front door.

Camille Jameson sighed in ecstasy and climbed back into her car. As she engaged the gears she laughed out loud and shouted, "Scarlett O'Hara, eat your heart out!"

That she had been hired to restore this mansion to its former glory was an intoxicating thought. She prayed silently that she would be able to meet the challenge. It was important to her career as a decorator and to her financial future.

Camille and her mother, Martha, owned a decorating business in Atlanta. Martha Jameson had tried to maintain it after Camille's father died, but by the time Camille had graduated from college with her decorator's degree, it had deteriorated into little more than a gift shop featuring undistinguished antiques and mediocre bric-a-brac. Camille soon began ordering contemporary decorating items and increasing the quality of the antiques they stocked. She offered her services as a consultant to customers who sought advice in their choice of wallpaper, carpet, draperies, furniture, and entire decorating schemes. Camille's good taste and easy, friendly manner had soon earned her a reputation and a respectable clientele. She now employed two other women who helped in the "studio," while her mother handled over-the-counter sales and the bookkeeping.

When Camille had been approached by Mr. Rayburn Prescott of Natchez, Mississippi, to redo his mansion, she jumped at the chance. This was by far her most important commission. She was well acquainted with the antebellum homes of old Natchez. She and her mother had toured the restored houses during one of the annual spring pilgrimages. Camille had been a young girl then, but those lovely homes had made a lasting impression on her.

Rayburn Prescott was the typical Southern gentleman, using courtly manners when addressing Camille or Martha. The other ladies in the studio had twittered when he spoke to them in a drawl more pronounced than they were accustomed to hearing even in Atlanta. His shock of white hair was still thick and waved away from a broad, high forehead. His blue eyes retained a sparkle, though he must have been approaching seventy. He was tall, stately, distinguished, and eloquent.

After the preliminaries of getting acquainted, he told Camille about his house in Natchez. "I'm ashamed of it, Miss Jameson. After my wife died, over twenty years ago, I let it fall into a sad state of disrepair. It has become a bachelor's house. My son spends most of his waking hours at our plantation across the river, but he agrees with me that we should restore Bridal Wreath to its original beauty."

"It has such a lovely name," Camille mused, already conjuring up pictures of the house in her mind. "I'll gladly accept your commission."

"But we haven't even talked about your fee or any of the details!" he exclaimed.

"It doesn't matter. I know I want to do it." She laughed at his surprised expression before his face crinkled into a pleasant smile. She had come highly recommended by a friend of his who owned a restaurant in Peachtree Plaza that Camille had decorated. Rayburn Prescott was convinced of her abilities. They talked about her fee and she was astounded at the sum he quoted. He gave her an almost limitless budget for the restoration. Apparently she wouldn't have to consciously economize. He insisted that she stay at Bridal Wreath during the restoration, promising that arrangements to that effect would be made for her. They set a mutually convenient date for her arrival, and now she was here, standing on the front porch, her purse under her arm, waiting for the bell she had rung to be answered. Upon close inspection, she noticed the chipping paint, the dulling rust that was corroding the brass appointments on the front door, and the warped boards waving the front porch beneath her feet. If the interior were as bad as the exterior, she had a lot of work to do.

Camille smiled wryly to herself. Work was *all* she had to do. Her life revolved around her career, much to the consternation of her mother and close friends, most of whom had husbands and several children. Her mother encouraged her to date the young men who stopped by the studio on contrived business, but Camille remained aloof to their advances. She passed off their flirtations as inconsequential, and Martha Jameson worried about her daughter's obvious lack of interest in the opposite sex.

It distressed Camille to see her mother so frustrated over her love life, or rather the lack of one, but she couldn't tell her the reason. She couldn't say, "Mother, I gave myself to a man once, and all I felt afterward was shame and humiliation. I don't intend to fall into that trap again." One didn't tell one's mother things like that. Besides, some memories were too painful to articulate. Camille shuddered and drew a long sigh at these recollections just as the front door opened. She looked into a smiling face.

"Hello. I'm Camille Jameson." She smiled, not knowing how fetching she looked with the sunlight bouncing off her dark, curly hair.

"Hello, Miss Jameson." The man's welcoming face was wreathed in smiles. "Mr. Prescott is waiting for you. He's as excited as a schoolboy going to his first dance. I'm sure glad you made the trip safely. He's been worried about a young lady like you driving herself all the way from Atlanta."

"I had no trouble on the trip, and I'm just as anxious to see Mr. Prescott again." She stepped into the entrance hall as the man moved aside. She glanced around her in awe. It was just as she hoped it would be!

"My name is Simon Mitchell, Miss Jameson. Any time you need anything, you call on me," the man said, drawing her attention momentarily away from her perusal of the house.

"Thank you, Mr. Mitchell." Her smile was genuine.

"Simon, please. Have a seat, Miss Jameson, and I'll go find Mr. Prescott. I think he's out back watering his plants."

"Take your time. I won't mind waiting." He nodded and moved toward the back of the house down the broad hall that ran its length. Camille longed to peer into the rooms that opened off the corridor, but felt she should wait for her host and new employer to show her through his home. Southerners like Rayburn Prescott were scrupulous about manners and etiquette.

She sat down on a chair in the hall and assumed the ladylike pose drilled into her by her mother: back straight, knees together, hands reposing gracefully in her lap. She suddenly wished she had a more refined look. She was cursed with dark, curly hair that she wore at a medium length so that on particularly humid days, she could pull it back into a chignon when only the tendrils around her face escaped into unruly curls. The dark hair was complemented by her apricot-toned skin. It wasn't dark enough to be called olive, and not rosy enough to be fair. Instead it glowed with the color of warm honey. She had always coveted her friends who had Dresden complexions that blushed becomingly. She saw no compensation in having skin that tanned to a dusky hue under the summer sun. And no one else on earth had eyes like hers. Why couldn't she have plain blue or green or hazel or even brown without those silly golden highlights in them? Other brown eyes were touched with a spark of hazel, or were mysteriously deep like ebony, but hers reflected gold in their depths. She hated them. Her long, dark lashes, wide, generous mouth, and pert nose had combined with her hair to give her a gypsy look. That had been her father's pet name for her—his little gypsy.

She couldn't help her features, so she saw to it that she was always dressed with utmost care. Her flair for color and design, which was so valuable to her vocation, went into her wardrobe, too. Now, she tugged the skirt of her yellow linen suit over her knees, wishing she might take off the jacket and wear only the cool, sheer print voile blouse underneath. The humidity in Natchez was wilting her clothes, not to mention what it was doing to her hair, which she had tamed into a semblance of control this morning. Now she knew it must be curling around her head in wild abandon.

She heard the crunch of tires on the driveway outside and then the loudly squeaking sound of a car door being slammed shut. She counted the three steps that she remembered leading up to the porch as someone took them quickly and then three more long steps across the front porch to the door. The knob on the door turned and it was flung open. It swung back and crashed into the wall before the looming figure standing silhouetted against the afternoon sun reached behind himself to close it. He stamped into the entrance hall, leaving muddy scuff marks on the parqueted oak floor. He moved with an easy gait that was vaguely familiar, but Camille was so infuriated with his negligent disregard for the abused floor, the door, and the wall, that she didn't give the familiarity a conscious thought. Before she reasoned against speaking out, she blurted, "It's no wonder this house is in such deplorable shape. If everyone who came in here was as careless as you are and as unappreciative of its beauty, it would be falling down within a week!"

The man stopped suddenly and glanced quickly around the hall, surprised by the feminine voice that was berating him. He had just come in from the blindingly bright sunlight, and it took a moment for him to adjust his eyes and spot her sitting in the shadows of the hallway. Without speaking, he removed his wide-brimmed straw hat and raked his arm across a perspiring forehead. Then, still holding his hat in one hand, he put both hands on his hips and looked at her fully for the first time.

"I beg your pardon," he said with deceptive calm, anger just below the surface. He took five steps forward and stopped within a few feet of her chair. Their gazes met and locked and there was a simultaneous sharp intake of breath from the two people staring at each other.

It couldn't be! He couldn't be here! What was he doing here? Is it him? Yes! No! It can't be! Camille's mouth had gone as dry as cotton and she tried convulsively to swallow. Her heart was pounding so hard she knew he must be able to see it stirring the fabric across her breasts. She flushed hot all over and then shivered with cold. The roaring in her ears was like a cannon blast. She knew by his stance and shocked expression that he was as dumbstruck as she.

He looked the same as he had in Utah almost two years ago. Maybe there were a few more web-like lines fanning out from the corners of his eyes, but the irises were as blue as ever, startling, piercing, hypnotizing. She knew all too well their hypnotic power! Was he taller? No. It must seem so because she was sitting down, but she knew that if she stood, she would still only reach his collarbone. He was as broad of shoulder and narrow of hip as she remembered. The physique that had been a part of her fantasies for these many months had not been exaggerated in her memory as she sometimes convinced herself that it was. His brown hair was streaked with sun-bleached strands. The tan skin drawn tightly over the lean lines of his face intensified the blue of his eyes, which studied her with the same hungry stare she felt in her own.

He wasn't dressed in the tight ski pants and soft sweaters she remembered. He wore western-cut jeans and cowboy boots—muddy boots that scuffed up floors. His blue chambray shirt was unbuttoned to the middle of his chest, the sleeves rolled to his elbows. It was damp and stained with perspiration. The hair on his arms and chest was bleached almost completely blond, and nestled in the curls on his chest was the gold ornament that Camille remembered tenderly. He told her the cross had belonged to his late mother. The chain that suspended it around his neck was heavy. In no way did the piece of jewelry look feminine, especially lying as it was in the damp hair of his chest.

"Zack Prescott?" She was barely able to verbalize his name. When Mr. Rayburn Prescott had introduced himself to her, said his name, she felt that sharp pang around her heart that accompanied any reminder of the skiing vacation she had taken after her graduation from college. She would never have imagined that those two men would be related. Zack had never told her where he called home. Had she ever asked? Had she cared?

"Don't I know you from somewhere?" He parroted the corny Hollywood line with all the sarcasm he could muster.

The tightness in Camille's throat relaxed long enough for her to say, "You told me you were a farmer, but I assumed you were joking." She tried to smile, but her lips were quivering. The muscles of her face wouldn't work.

The lines on either side of his mouth hardened. "What else did you 'assume' about me? I'd be curious to know."

The bitterness underlying his words stung Camille, and she flinched. Then the familiar regrets that had haunted her for days, months, years came back and with them the guilt and shame he had caused her to suffer. Anger flared from the golden depths of her eyes as she snarled,

"What do you think I assumed about a man who so heartlessly seduced an innocent girl."

"No less than he assumed about a *woman* so easily seduced." His words fell on her like physical blows and she catapulted out of the chair to stand directly in front of him.

"You . . . you're hateful and immoral, without conscience. I despise you for what you did to me—"

"You have an unconvincing way of displaying your aversion, Camille," he interrupted her, and she wanted to slap his arrogant face. But the sound of her name coming from those full, soft, sensual lips halted any action she would have taken. She had the overwhelming compulsion to reach out and stroke his lean, brown cheek. She clenched her fists to stymie the impulse. They stared at each other for a long moment before they heard Simon's footsteps coming down the hall. Camille whirled away from Zack and tried vainly to compose her features.

"Miss Jameson, Mr. Prescott will see you now. Hello, Zack. Have you met Miss Jameson?" Camille had her back to him, and Zack must have nodded in acknowledgment, for he didn't speak. "Well then, you come with me, Miss Jameson, and Zack can join you for refreshments later. Mr. Prescott hopes you don't mind meeting him on the terrace."

"N-no, that's fine." Anything to get away from

the disturbing presence behind her. She followed Simon down the hall without looking back.

They crossed a large screened back porch that extended the length of the house and allowed an unobstructed view of the grounds. Simon held a screened door open for Camille and she stepped out onto the brick terrace. Mr. Rayburn Prescott gallantly rose from his wicker chair and came toward her, his arms outstretched.

He grasped both her hands in his. "Miss Jameson, what a pleasure it is to look at you. Welcome to Bridal Wreath." He spoke with the soft and melodious voice Camille remembered. She returned his deep smile, almost forgetting the shattering experience of seeing Zack just a moment before.

"Thank you, Mr. Prescott, but please call me Camille. I love your home. It's even more wonderful than I expected it to be."

He shook his head sorrowfully. "If Alice, my late wife, could see it, I'm afraid she would be very angry with me. I went into an abysmal depression for years after I lost her. Zachary, my son, was some comfort, but no one could replace her in my life. I concentrated on the plantation and it prospered as a result, but since I did little entertaining except for an occasional poker game, I let the house run down. That's why I hired you to restore it for me. We have all the modern conveniences, of course, but it needs to be redecorated. I have every confidence in your abilities."

His smile was kind and gentle as he led her to a glass-topped table where a frosted pitcher of lemonade and several glasses shimmered in the dappled sunlight that filtered through the large shade trees. He held a chair for her and offered her a glass of lemonade with an inclination of his head. She accepted by nodding.

Looking around her at the lovely grounds, better maintained here than the ones in front of the house, she wondered how she was going to tell him that it would be impossible for her to accept his commission. She wouldn't be able to live and work at Bridal Wreath, be near the one person in the world whom she had never wanted to see again. She couldn't live with the chance of meeting Zack several times a day as they came and went about their business and be submitted to that flush of acute embarrassment every time she looked at him, realizing that he remembered well the last time they were together. She couldn't do it! But how could she tell this old gentleman that she must disappoint him in order to retain her own sanity? She felt compelled to leave his house and his son as soon as possible, now, today. The thought was a crushing one. What would this do to her career? How could she sacrifice such an incredible opportunity?

"Do you like my garden?" Mr. Prescott's question brought her back from her reverie as he gestured to take in the broad expanse of lawn. "I take pride in my plants. Since I'm no longer able to work in the fields of the plantation—Zack has adamantly refused that I so much as cross the river—I spend as much time with these plants as I can. I have some outstanding tomatoes over there." He pointed to the plants that were growing in large redwood tubs at the corner of the terrace and Camille responded with genuine praise.

"They *do* look outstanding. I've never seen any larger, and I'll bet they taste just as good as they look."

He beamed. "We'll have some for dinner. I'm rather proud of them. I enjoy growing food, but I love my flowers, too."

Camille glanced around at the myriad flowerbeds, hanging baskets, and urns, each boasting its own variety of flowering plant. They bloomed in profusion, in a rainbow of colors. The ferns growing in wire baskets hanging from the branches of trees by long chains were lush and three times Camille's arm span. It looked like a tropical paradise.

"I think you'll miss working outdoors when the weather starts growing cooler, won't you?" she asked perceptively.

He nodded his white head. "Yes, but then Simon and I work on our house plants. We take most of these ferns and tropicals inside. Zack accuses me of trying to move him out when the house is so crowded with plants." He offered her more lemonade, but she declined. He was so generous and sweet. How was she going to do what she must gracefully?

He had referred to Zack by name three times since they had sat down. Why hadn't he mentioned him in Atlanta? She would have known the name readily enough, for it was never far from her thoughts. She could have contrived some excuse to refuse the job and avoided any unpleasantness.

She was perspiring and could feel her hair escaping the small amount of control she had sprayed on it earlier from an aerosol can. She must look frightful. Her nervousness at what she had to tell him didn't help. She licked her lips and raised her eyes to his. "Mr. Prescott, I'm afraid there's something—"

"There you are, Zack! Come meet our houseguest." Rayburn Prescott's eyes were looking over her head and she heard the unmistakable tread of cowboy boots coming closer.

"Camille Jameson, I want you to meet my son, Zack."

Camille was studying the purse clutched tightly in her lap, but glanced up at the man who stood so close to her chair. "We met, Dad." Zack paused significantly, then added, "Out in the hallway."

"Good, good. Would you like some lemonade?"

"Yes, please. It's hotter than—"

"Zack! Remember we're going to have a lady around here from now on," Rayburn chided him.

"Of course. Please excuse me." Zack executed a mocking bow to Camille. "Aren't you warm, Miss Jameson? Let me help you with your jacket."

Before Camille could accept or refuse, he slipped behind her and placed his large, masculine hands on her shoulders. She tingled at his touch and wanted to scream in frustrated anger that he still had the power to make her tremble with alarming sensations. His fingers tightened on her shoulders and his hands remained there longer than necessary before he slid the jacket from her shoulders, following it with his hands down her arms until her fingers slipped out of the sleeves. He draped the jacket over the back of her chair before taking a chair across from her. She mumbled a "thank you" before she raised her eyes.

He had showered, and damp hair fell over his forehead. He had forsaken the western work jeans for a clean, starched pair with a designer label on the hip pocket. They fit his taut hips and muscled thighs far too well. The eyes fixed on her were vivid blue and full of sardonic amusement. He was enjoying this predicament! He wanted her to feel ashamed and embarrassed! He was a cad of the worst sort. He used women for his own pleasure and then was contemptuously delighted at their shame. She straightened her shoulders and flashed him a look of pure venom before she returned her attention to Rayburn, who was totally unaware of the undercurrents of tension between his son and his new employee.

Camille tried to catch the last of what he had been saying. ". . . know you have excellent taste and will do a good job, and I for one wouldn't presume to tell you how to do your work."

"What Dad is trying to say, Miss Jameson," Zack cut in, "is that we don't want the house to look like some fairy-decorated Bourbon Street bordello."

"Zachary, that is no way to talk to a lady. You have been around the field hands too long," his father remonstrated.

"I apologize, Miss Jameson," Zack's words sounded sincere, but the look he gave her revealed that he didn't think she was a lady at all. She was further insulted when his gaze moved from her eyes to her chest. The sheer voile blouse could have vanished under his intent stare and Camille wouldn't have felt any more exposed. Did he remember what she looked like under her clothes? Or had he taken so many women since then that he had long forgotten her? Either way, she wished he wouldn't look at her with that smug, knowing expression on his face. She had a mad desire to reach for her jacket and cover herself.

She blushed a deep peach color and apparently the elder Mr. Prescott thought her discomfort was due to the heat because he said, "Forgive us,

Camille, but you must be tired and hot after your trip. We can go over the rest of the details after dinner. Right now, you need to rest. You'll be staying in what we call the dowager house." He indicated a small apartment across the terrace from the main house. "It's a presumptuous name, I'll concede, but my wife's mother lived with us for several years after we married and insisted she stay under a separate roof. She made what was once a carriage house into a comfortable apartment. At least I hope you find it to be. She gave it that name and it's stuck all these years."

Camille couldn't look at Zack. Her heart was pounding and she dreaded the next few minutes, but she had to get it over with. The sooner, the better. she couldn't let this kind old man go on thinking she was going to stay here and do what he had hired her to do. She was thankful no money had exchanged hands yet and that she had not ordered materials for the restoration.

She stared at the empty glass in front of her and followed with her eyes a small bead of moisture as it rolled to the bottom of the glass and became part of a pool forming there. "Mr. Prescott, I don't know how to tell you—"

"Miss Jameson, let me add my enthusiasm to that of my father's. He has been wanting to do this project for several months, and is anxious to get started on it. He was very excited about putting his plans into action, hiring you, and I'm certain that you are just as eager to begin the restoration as he is. *As soon as possible.*" Zack's last four words cut through her like a knife. She looked at him quickly and saw a threatening expression on his chiseled face. He had sensed she was about to back out of the deal and was warning her not to. Why? "As soon as possible." Understanding began to dawn as she looked back at Mr. Prescott. He was gazing benignly across the yard, lost in his own thoughts. Though he had been sitting for the past few minutes, his breathing seemed to be rapid and shallow, his face mottled as if he had been running. Camille swallowed a lump in her throat as she turned back to Zack. She raised her eyebrows in a silent query and almost imperceptibly he nodded his head. She slumped in her chair, deflated by this new turn of events. What was she to do? Must she stay here and be subject to Zack's constant contempt? She had agreed to do a job for Mr. Rayburn Prescott. If he were in bad health, she was dutybound to see that job completed. What had happened between her and Zack had nothing to do with her present obligation to his father. She would have to push thoughts of Zack out of her mind and be impervious to his sarcasm. Maybe they wouldn't be seeing as much of each other as she anticipated. Maybe.

Rayburn realized that a silence had settled over the three of them and roused himself. "Zack, where are your manners? I'll escort Camille to her apartment, and you bring her bags."

Camille's decision had been made for her.

She fished the car keys out of her purse and dropped them into Zack's palm, avoiding touching him. She ignored his mocking grin. "There are several sample books in the car, too. Just leave them and I'll get them later."

His grin faded and he seemed irritated. "Where do you want them?"

"What?"

"The sample books."

"In . . . in the hallway, I guess."

He nodded and rapidly strode across the terrace and around the corner of the house. She took Rayburn's proffered arm and they walked toward the dowager house. She liked that silly name. He opened the door for her as they stepped inside. Though it wasn't air conditioned, there was a large ceiling fan circulating the air and making the small apartment cool. The drone of the fan would be nice to sleep to, Camille thought. The main room wasn't large, but as promised, very comfortable. The furnishings and appointments were old-fashioned and dated themselves, but Camille wouldn't have traded them for the sterile environment of a hotel room. The bed was a lovely rosewood four-poster. The deep fringe of the ecru chenille spread draped to the floor. White sheer curtains were all that covered the windows, and Camille was glad to see that there were window shades that could be pulled down for privacy at night.

"Is it all right?" Rayburn asked anxiously. His eagerness to make her feel welcome was touching.

She rested a hand on his arm and answered, "It's lovely, thank you."

He smiled down at her. "The small kitchen is there"—he indicated a corner—"though we expect you to take all your meals with us in the main house. The refrigerator is stocked with juice and cold drinks. If you need anything else, ask Simon. The bath is through there, and this is the closet." He crossed the room and opened the door. A fragrant smell permeated the room. Camille followed him and peeked over his shoulder. He laughed.

"It's a cedar closet. My mother-in-law had it put in when she furnished the apartment."

He closed the closet door and took both of her hands again, holding them between his calloused palms. "I'm glad you're here, Camille. You can't know how much I want to do this project. Zack thinks it's the fanciful indulgence of an old man and that I'm doing it for myself, but I'm really doing it for him. I had hoped that Zack would marry and raise children in this rambling old house. I've just about given up hope of ever seeing my grandchildren. I wish that by having the house restored, he'll start thinking about a family. I'll feel better about . . . leaving . . . if I know he's settled. Of course, this is our secret." He winked at her.

"Of course," she strangled out.

He patted her hands. "Now, I must go so you

can rest before dinner. It's at eight o'clock. Zack will be along shortly with your luggage. Make yourself at home." He smiled at her one more time before he shut the door behind him.

Camille made a cursory inspection of the small kitchen and bathroom. The fan made flickering shadows on the pastel walls as it rotated lazily. The sheer curtains billowed into the room with a small breath of breeze. Camille kicked off her shoes and tossed her purse onto the rosewood chest of drawers. She placed her watch and bracelet beside it and was removing her earrings when one of them dropped out of her hand and rolled under the bed. She scrambled after it, falling to her hands and knees, her back to the door. She was squinting into the darkness under the bed with her cheek resting on the floor when she heard Zack say behind her, "Nice view."

She jumped up quickly and turned to face him, pushing errant curls away from her flushed face. "A gentleman would have knocked before coming in," she raged.

He shrugged, not in the least disturbed by her anger. "Alas, my hands were full." He held a piece of luggage in each of his hands.

"That's no excuse. You could have called out."

"Yes, I could have," he admitted unrepentantly. He smiled at her wickedly and Camille wished she didn't feel so isolated and unprotected here with him. She watched him warily as he placed her large bag near the closet and then took her smaller one into the bathroom, guessing correctly that it contained her cosmetics. *Well, he certainly makes himself at home, doesn't he?* She was jealous of his apparent calm when inside she was in turmoil. His casual cotton shirt was opened to the middle of his chest, and as he handled the heavy bags, Camille didn't fail to notice how the muscles of his shoulders and arms rippled under the fabric. The fan overhead stirred the sun-bleached brown curls on his head.

"Service with a smile, ma'am," he drawled as he came back from the bathroom and tossed her keys onto the chest. "I can't help but wonder who carried your bags that night you ran away from Snow Bird. They must have been heavy, packed as they were with all of your ski clothes. Were you in such a hurry to leave that you managed them on your own? I would have thought you would have been too tired for that much exertion." He was smiling, but his voice was bitter, his eyes blue ice.

"Please, Zack, for all our sakes, let's not refer to when we . . . met before," she pleaded. "It will be better for everyone."

"Oh, I'm sure it will be better for you, coward that you are. You were about to run again, weren't you? Out there on the terrace, you were preparing to make a nice little speech declining my father's commission."

"Yes," she confessed. "The possibility that Mr.

Rayburn Prescott was related to . . . to you . . . never crossed my mind. I thought . . . hoped . . . I'd never see you again. I didn't feel like I should stay under the circumstances, but I can tell the restoration is important to him. And I had already agreed to do it."

"Well, for whatever your reasons, I'm glad you decided to stay." He said the words grudgingly, as if not wanting to credit her with having done anything good or noble.

Ignoring the sharp pain that came with knowing what he must truly think of her, she asked, "Is he ill, Zack?"

"Yes," he answered succinctly. He turned away from her and stared out the wide windows. "He had a heart attack last year and he's never been completely well since. The doctors don't give him a very good prognosis. When he started talking about wanting to restore the house, I encouraged the idea. He needs a project and this place means so much to him. Whatever amount of money it takes to get it back in shape for him, I'm more than willing to spend."

It's a legacy for you, Zack, she wanted to tell him, but of course, she couldn't.

Zack continued. "He told me about hiring a decorator in Atlanta. He spoke very highly of your professional abilities and his impressions of you as a person. He never told me your name. I never thought to ask it. It didn't seem important as long as he was pleased." He remained with his back to her as he added slowly, "I was as surprised as you when I saw you today and heard your audacious scolding of me in my own house." He turned back to her then and shrugged, a twisted smile on his face.

"I'll do a good job for him, Zack, I promise. In spite of our former . . . relationship." She whispered the last word, embarrassed at the intimacy it implied.

His stern face seemed to soften, or it could have been only the play of shadows across it. He muttered, "Thank you, Camille," before he left hurriedly.

Two

Camille showered and slipped into a light robe. She didn't pull down the window shades for fear of blocking out what little breeze there was, but she lay down on the bed hoping that anyone passing by wouldn't be able to see into her room. The sheets on the bed were cool and fragrant. She stretched, pointing her toes and constricting each muscle in her body. She relaxed them slowly, enjoying relief from the tension that had been building since she arrived and saw Zack Prescott in the hallway of the main house.

She never, even in her wildest imaginings, had expected to see the man again. His being owner and resident of Bridal Wreath, which she had been commissioned to restore, put her in an untenable situation. How was she going to handle it? It would be easy to run away, as Zack had shrewdly guessed she was planning to do. That had been her first instinct, but now she knew she couldn't take so drastic an action. For one thing, deserting an important job like this wouldn't be good for her career. She needed a major project like this to use for future reference. The money she would make was too much to ignore. Rayburn Prescott had trusted her and obviously thought well of her, and she didn't want to disappoint him, especially in light of the fact that he was seriously ill. How would she explain declining the commission to her mother? Certainly not by telling her the truth. And if she were honest with herself, she didn't want Zack to have the satisfaction of driving her off. He would love to gloat over the fact that she had run away again. He would assume that she couldn't take the pressure, that she had retreated from an adult situation. No! She wasn't going to give him the pleasure. *I'm going to stay and do my work and ignore him as much as possible.*

Camille turned her face into the pillow and sobbed, for she knew that very few women could ignore a man like Zachary Prescott. Hadn't she been unable to resist him in Utah?

She sighed. As much as she hated the memories and tried to secure them in a dim recess of her mind, they pushed themselves to the forefront, where she was forced to face them. She relaxed her conscious control and surrendered to the sweet pain of memory. She remembered Utah . . . remembered Snow Bird . . . remembered Zack . . .

The ski trip had been a surprise graduation present from her mother. Camille had felt guilty knowing how much money it must have cost and was reluctant to accept it from her widowed and financially struggling mother, but all the arrangements had been made and Martha insisted. Besides, two of Camille's friends were going, too. The girls' parents had met secretly and planned this winter fling for them since the coeds were graduating at the end of the fall term.

Kathy Grayson and Jan Murphy were two of Camille's sorority sisters and they had spent hours together in their dormitory rooms dreaming of adventures such as this trip was expected to be. Kathy and Jan were going as experienced skiers, and were more interested in the prospects of meeting eligible young men than the conditions of the slopes. Camille had never skied, and was both excited and anxious about learning how.

Snow Bird resort, an hour's drive from Salt Lake City, was everything they could have anticipated. The three young women checked into their rooms at the lodge with high spirits, calling back and forth between the connecting rooms about the man they had seen on the elevator, their plans for dinner, and most importantly, what they would wear.

Kathy and Jan met two men from California that first night at dinner. Camille was more cautious about forming any kind of attachment with a stranger. She had many male friends at college and had had a few romances, some heartbreaking, some nice, but she had never been able to fall in and out of love with the careless regularity that most of her friends did.

She concentrated on her skiing the first two days, taking lessons on the elementary slopes and feeling like a clumsy oaf while Kathy and Jan raced down the mountains with their two agile Californians.

Every muscle in her body ached in angry protest of her abuse of it, and there were few spots on her hips and thighs where ugly purple bruises weren't evident. Was she made for this kind of sport? Everyone else seemed to love it. She must be a freak.

She winced as she sat down at a table in the lodge dining room for dinner. It was the evening of the second day. Kathy and Jan had gone into Salt Lake City with their young men for dinner, and though they had pleaded with her to come along, she begged off. She didn't wish to be a fifth wheel, and wanted only to eat quickly and then go to her room and soak in a hot tub until some of the soreness was eased from her battered body.

She hadn't expected anyone to speak to her and jumped when she heard Zack's voice behind her ask if she were alone and if she would like some company for dinner. Turning to look at the source of such an interesting voice, she was immediately arrested by the brightness of his blue eyes. His smile was soft and easy, his clothes impeccable; he was gorgeous. Had he made a mistake? Was this man—a man several years older than she—asking her to share dinner with him?

She stammered some inane reply and he took a seat across from her. The next several minutes she was never able to recall. She was so shaken by him and his commanding presence that later she hoped she had conversed with at least a modicum of intelligence. Soon, however, his amicable manner became contagious and they were chatting companionably about movies, books, and skiing.

His accent was obviously Southern, and when she asked him what he did as his occupation, he laughed and told her he was a farmer. She had thought he was joking and laughed with him and they went on to another subject. He graciously invited her to dance, but she refused, admitting that she was too sore for anything more physically stimulating than eating her dinner. When they were done, they talked over cups of cappuccino in front of the giant fireplace at one end of the dining room, and then he escorted her to her door.

"Will you be on the slopes tomorrow?"

"I think I'll be in better shape by then. I hope so," she laughed, flexing a muscle.

His smile and manner were so engaging that she laughed again in sheer joy. "Thank you for sharing your table with me tonight, Camille. I'll probably see you tomorrow on the mountain." He took her hand briefly in his, then turned and walked with casual ease down the hall toward the elevator.

Camille was unaccountably and irritatingly nervous the next morning and wore her most attractive ski suit. She chided herself for behaving like a teen-ager with a wild crush on the captain of the football team, but at breakfast, despite her resolve not to, she searched the room for his face.

It wasn't until almost noon when she first saw him. He flew past her with lightning speed and then deftly plowed himself to a stop and waited for her to catch up. She hated for him to witness her less than expert maneuvers.

"Good morning," he called cheerfully. His hair was shining in the bright sunlight, windblown and casual. His physique was disturbingly revealed in the tight ski pants, and his eyes were mirrors of the sapphire Utah sky.

For the rest of the day he was never far away from her. She would turn, unexpectedly catch him watching her, and return his smile. When he came by her table and spoke to her at lunch, Kathy and Jan nearly choked on their Reuben sandwiches.

"Is he a movie star? My God, he's beautiful. Camille, what happened last night? Have you been holding out on us? Tell us all the details."

Camille was embarrassed by their overzealous interest, and even more embarrassed by the fact that there was really nothing to tell. He had been polite and that was all there was to it.

She ate dinner with the depressed twosome, whose gentleman friends had left for home that afternoon. When dinner was over and the small dance band began to play, Zack presented himself and asked Camille to dance. She stepped into his arms, trying to ignore the raised eyebrows of her two friends and hoping desperately that Zack hadn't noticed their curious stares.

He held her against him with more assurance than any man ever had. She felt powerless in his strong arms and it was a heady, intoxicating feeling. He danced gracefully, as he did everything else, and Camille surrendered to his able lead. Once he moved his chin in her dark hair and she thought he murmured something, but she may have been mistaken. When he released her and led her back to the table, she covered her disappointment with a tremulous smile.

He strolled over to her after breakfast the next morning and greeted Kathy and Jan with a heart-melting smile.

"I see a notice on the bulletin board announcing a hayride tonight. Would you like to go, Camille?"

"Yes." She smiled back. "That sounds like fun." She sounded so composed, but her heart was in her throat.

"Good. I'll pick you up at your room a few minutes before nine."

They waved to each other throughout the day when they chanced to meet on the slopes. He wasn't at dinner in the lodge, but Camille finished quickly and went to her room to dress for the hayride. She wore a pair of tight jeans she considered flattering to her figure and stuffed the legs into her knee-high boots. A soft, yellow angora sweater topped them. In this feminine mood, she refused to wear the insulated underwear she had been wearing under her ski clothes and hoped she would be warm enough.

She watched Zack covertly as they rode down the elevator after he called for her. He, too, was dressed in jeans. Well-worn cowboy boots peeked out from the frayed hems of his pants' legs. Under a shearling coat, he had on a white cable knit sweater. The fingers that pushed the buttons on the elevator panel were long and strong. The back of his hand was tanned and sprinkled with light blond hair.

Before they went out into the cold air to climb aboard the horse-drawn wagon, he pulled her toward him and with confident fingers drew the edges of her rabbit fur parka together, lined up the bottom of the zipper, and eased it up slowly over her chest to just under her chin.

"I don't want you to catch a cold," he whispered, and Camille trembled at his confident intimacy.

They sat in the sweet-smelling hay, huddled

under blankets provided by the lodge. When everyone started singing, Camille smiled as his soft baritone caressed her and his warm breath fanned her cheek.

He put his arm around her and drew her closer to him, though their legs were already entwined for warmth. She was shocked when he unzipped her parka a few inches and put the hand that had been settled on her shoulder inside and rested it against the base of her throat. Her pulse began to race when his fingers played along her collarbone and stroked her neck. When she glanced up at him timidly, he only smiled and leaned forward to kiss her lightly on the forehead.

Snow was just beginning to fall when the wagon returned to the lodge. Zack lifted her down, and Camille started up the steps of the building. His fingers wrapped around her elbow and he gently pulled her back.

"I can make a mean cup of cappuccino. Would you come to my room and share one with me? Please?"

His voice was compelling, his smile tender, and Camille exercised no resistance against the combination of them, though alarm bells were sounding warnings in her brain. She nodded mutely and linked her arm in his. They strolled down the icy paths of the compound to another group of buildings. These were the condominiums, and Zack explained that a friend of his owned one and had lent it to him. He unlocked the door to one of the units and they stepped inside. The room was distinctly masculine. Rough, wide beams were exposed across the tall, sloping ceiling. At one side of the room a large picture window opened upon a vista of the mountains. A small kitchen was behind louvered doors, and Camille reasoned that the other door led to the bathroom. A stone fireplace took up another wall and directly opposite it was a king-sized bed with a suede bedspread thrown across it.

To cover her nervousness Camille remarked, "This is apparently the high-rent district. My room in the lodge is nice, but nothing like this."

He helped her out of her parka and laid it in a chair. "Yes. My friend doesn't have any money problems. I doubt if he's been here more than a couple of times. Go sit by the fire and I'll make our drinks."

He went whistling into the kitchen. He seemed accustomed to being alone with a woman in what was little more than a glamorous bedroom. Camille crossed to the window and studied the landscape, listening to him clattering utensils in the kitchen.

"It's snowing harder. I'm glad it held off until after the hayride." Unconsciously, she drew the cord that closed the drapes.

He tried to suppress a smile at her action as he came back carrying two steaming mugs. She felt like a ninny. Shutting the drapes indeed! Would he think she was desiring privacy from the outside world? Was she?

He drew her down beside him on the rug before the fire and removed her damp boots, massaging her toes back to life before he pulled off his own boots and stretched his feet toward the fire.

They chatted about inconsequential things and laughed at one man on the hayride who couldn't carry a tune, but sang louder than anyone and kept getting everyone else confused.

When they finished their cappuccino, and the trivial conversation used to soothe the mounting tension between them ceased, he took her cup and set it aside with his. He faced her and slid both hands behind her neck, drawing her face to his.

The lips that met hers were warm and persuasive, moving over hers with a developed technique, tenderly demanding that she respond. When her tongue first touched his, an electric current shot through her and she wrapped her arms around his back. She had fantasized kissing him, but she wasn't prepared for the impact his embrace had on her. The kiss was tender, but masterful. She didn't feel plundered, but rather discovered.

Hot, fervent kisses traveled over her face and neck and she never knew how he managed to divest her of her sweater. He gazed derisively at the glossy fabric of her sheer brassiere, which made her breasts look more naked than if they had been bare.

"That's not doing much good, is it?" he chuckled as he unclasped the front fastener.

His hands knew what they were about and stirred her in a way that none of the aggravating, schoolboy fumblings of other men had done. He buried his face between her breasts and murmured, "Camille. Camille, you're so sweet. And beautiful. And I want to make love to you."

Had she agreed with a nod or had she spoken or had he considered a long silence her acquiescence? She didn't remember. He carried her to the bed and threw back the suede spread. She must have removed her jeans when he turned his back to remove his own clothing, for the next thing she knew they were lying together naked under the smooth sheets. His body was beautiful. The firelight danced around the room and bathed the hair on his chest, arms, and legs with a golden light.

"Camille," he breathed, stroking her breasts. He fastened his mouth to hers and she was powerless to do anything but meet his passion. His lovemaking was tender and fierce. He carried her with him on a passionate quest and when the culmination came, Camille's preconceived notions of how it would be diminished with the splendor of the actuality.

When he finally pushed away from her, he brushed the damp curls from her temples and searched her amber eyes. "You should have told me, Camille. I'm sorry."

She lay languidly in his arms, enjoying the steady beat of his heart under her ear. "Are you?" she whispered.

"No," he laughed softly. But he pulled her closer, stroking her body gently as he buried his face in her hair. "Why didn't you say something?"

She raised herself up and looked at him incredulously. "Well, it isn't something you just drop into a casual conversation. 'Isn't it a lovely day? Oh, by the way, I've never been to bed with a man before.' What would you have done if I'd said that?"

"Probably what I did anyway." He dropped his eyes to her breasts. "I couldn't have resisted you." He kissed her again deeply, then turned her on her side and placed her back against his chest and stomach. "Go to sleep." He nuzzled her ear and laid his head down beside hers on the same pillow.

Camille never slept that night. She listened to his even breathing and knew that he slept, but she was too excited to sleep. His warm breath stirred her hair. His hand rested possessively on her hip. She felt warm, relaxed, and secure. At home. At peace. Fulfilled.

As inexperienced as she was, she had been gratified to hear his small cries of pleasure. She had pleased him.

Something about those words grated on her as

an unwelcome thought bounced around her brain. Was that all it had been to him? A pleasure trip? All the signs pointed to the fact that he was skilled in the art of lovemaking. He probably had to fight women off. Camille now realized that she had certainly offered him no resistance. She had come willingly into his arms, his bed! Then she began to count all the things she knew about him. Nothing! Nothing except his name and that he had a wealthy friend who owned this bed she was sharing so wantonly. He hadn't plagued her with a multitude of questions about herself either. He didn't want to know. He didn't care! He had shared a few fun days and one night with a woman ten years his junior whose inexperience must have been a novelty to him. Camille felt dirty and ashamed. His loving had been tender and gentle, and seemingly genuine, but she was sure that was part of his game plan to woo her.

She shivered at another horrifying thought. Pregnancy! My God! She didn't take pills or use any other contraceptives and he hadn't either. What if, even now, she was carrying this stranger's baby!

A deeper, more disturbing thought flashed unbidden through her brain and it was more absurd and frightening than any of its predecessors. She couldn't give credence to that. No!

She panicked. She ran.

She extricated herself from his warm embrace,

painstakingly striving not to awaken him. She gathered her clothes and dressed with fumbling fingers. After quietly letting herself out the door, she ran through the snowstorm to the lodge and demanded that the sleepy clerk prepare her bill and arrange for her transportation back to Salt Lake City. She assured him that it was an emergency when he hedged about traversing the mountain pass in a snowstorm. She avoided his probing, curious eyes.

In her room she packed her bags quickly, sobbing as she did so. She scrawled a hasty note to her friends, who would surely be alarmed over her sudden departure. She lied and said that her mother had called and an old family friend had taken sick and was not expected to live. The tale sounded ludicrous, even to her, but it was the best her fractured mind could come up with.

She fled into the night, arriving at the airport in Salt Lake City just as dawn was breaking, thankful that the old station wagon and the sleepy chauffeur who had driven it had made the trip safely. She caught the first airplane going east with a connecting flight to Atlanta.

This was the middle of September in Natchez, Mississippi. Those events had taken place in December on a snowy Utah mountain. It would soon be two years ago. Zack Prescott had haunted her ever since that night.

Thinking about it all now, she recalled that just before she left him, she had glanced toward the bed where he lay sleeping. His masculine form had been outlined by the soft sheet, his hair lay in tousled disarray on his forehead, and dark lashes rested on lean cheeks. A gnawing pain akin to hunger had almost altered her decision to flee then.

She felt that same pain now.

Three

Camille dressed for dinner with great care. She had brought to Natchez a white eyelet sundress, knowing that she would be able to wear it only once or twice before the lateness of the season forced her to store it away until next spring. It was one of her favorite dresses and, as she privately conceded, one of her most flattering. Two wide straps tied around her neck in a halter, leaving her back bare, and showing her tan to advantage. The neckline was discreetly plunging and the waist was gathered with a wide, jade green satin belt.

Camille had never liked her figure and had wept daily during her teen years when other girls began to show womanly curves. She had remained slender and only since young womanhood developed a generous bustline while retaining slim hips and thighs. Now she was envied by most of her peers who, after one or two babies, were finding it difficult, if not impossible, to match Camille's youthful figure.

She sprayed perfume from an atomizer and watched the fragrant mist settle on the soft curls surrounding her face and brushing her shoulders. She had decided to let her hair go "natural." Why fight it? In this Natchez humidity, any control on the curly tresses was temporary and futile.

Her heart leapt to her throat when she spotted Zack's reflection in the mirror. He stood silhouetted beyond the screened door behind her. Camille had assumed she would walk over to the main house alone. It had never occurred to her that she would be provided an escort.

He raised his hand and knocked with deliberate emphasis. She flushed angrily at his mocking insolence.

"You may as well come in, Zack. How long have you been standing there?"

"That will give you something to worry about. I'll admit that I haven't been bored." His smile was leering and Camille turned back to the mirror to put small pearl earrings into her pierced ears.

"I'm ready," she mumbled. Why did he look so gorgeous? His cream-colored linen suit and baby blue shirt, which was open at the collar, emphasized his tan and the cerulean brilliance of his eyes. When he smiled his teeth were startling white in the dark face.

"Not quite. My father sent the lady a corsage

made of buds from his own rose beds. I've been instructed to see that you wear them."

He extended a small corsage of yellow roses tied with a white satin ribbon. "How lovely of him," Camille exclaimed in a genuine feminine reaction to receiving flowers.

"Dearly, our housekeeper and Simon's wife, made it up for him, but he picked the roses himself. He is completely smitten by you."

Camille sniffed the delicate blossoms and raised her eyes to Zack's. She was surprised to find him looking at her closely. The expression on his face was strange and Camille couldn't quite name the emotion registered there, but it was immediately replaced by one of derision as her eyes met his.

"I'll have to wear the corsage in my hair, I suppose. I don't have a pin that will hold it onto my dress."

With the flourish of a magician pulling a rabbit out of a hat, Zack flipped back the lapel of his coat and produced a long straight pin with a pearl tip. "I was a Boy Scout. I came prepared."

He took the corsage from her and, before she realized what he was going to do, slipped his fingers between her and the fabric of her dress. The touch of his warm hands against her flesh acted as a catalyst that set her heart racing, made breathing difficult, and sent a warm flush radiating out from the pit of her stomach and encompassing her whole body. Did she imagine that Zack's fingers trembled slightly when they pressed into the top of her breast as he adjusted the pin behind the corsage? The flowers were secured, yet he made no move to extract his hand and she could feel his ragged breath on the top of her head. Slowly, she raised her eyes and took in the hair on his chest, the strong column of neck, the stubborn chin, the sensuous mouth, the long, slender nose and finally the blue eyes that pierced her with an alarming intensity. Her face was inches from his, but she felt an invisible barrier between them that neither of them was willing to breach. She quickly lowered her eyes and leaned away from him.

With a muttered oath, Zack jerked his hand out of her bodice. It was an abrupt movement and, in his haste, he had not been careful of the pin. It painfully pricked his finger.

"Damn," he cursed as he examined the pinprick that sported a bright red bead of blood.

Camille acted instinctively and grabbed his hand. "Oh, Zack," she cried. She brought his finger to her lips and sucked gently on it as she would have done her own had it been pricked. His sharp intake of breath brought it home to her what she was doing and the intimacy of it. She took his finger from between her lips and looked down on the wound that could barely be seen now. She released his hand as if it had burned her. "I . . . I think it will . . . will be okay now," she stammered. She didn't meet his eyes.

He crossed to the door and held it open for her as she scrambled past him.

After drinks in the parlor, Camille and her hosts enjoyed a leisurely dinner in the dining room. It was served by a bustling woman whom Rayburn introduced as Dearly Beloved Mitchell. She and Simon had served as housekeeper and butler-valet for Bridal Wreath ever since Rayburn had first brought his bride there.

At Camille's startled reaction to her name, Rayburn explained that Dearly's mother had liked the sound of the two opening words of the wedding ceremony so much that she gave them to her first child. "I'm just glad I was a girl child!" the smiling woman joked. She was as plump as Simon was slender but shared his pleasant, sunny personality. Camille liked them both immediately.

"Miss Jameson, you're as pretty as Mr. Prescott told me you were," Dearly continued. "The way he carried on about you, I was beginning to wonder if his intentions at having you stay here and work on the house were entirely honorable." She laughed happily at Rayburn's flushed face. The housekeeper, who apparently felt secure enough in her position in the household to tease her employers, added, "Now, if he had said he was bringing you here for Zack's appraisal, I would have understood perfectly." She laughed heartily again and disappeared through a door that Camille assumed led into the kitchen. She risked looking toward Zack, who was scowling darkly into his highball glass.

"Camille, please excuse Dearly and her sassy tongue. Over the years we have become accustomed to her outspoken opinions." Rayburn smiled at her and she assured him that she had taken no offense.

Dearly returned with several trays laden with covered dishes and set them on the table. When Camille had heaped her plate, she forked a piece of delicious-looking roast beef.

"Perhaps I should warn you, Camille, that in deference to my diet, Dearly doesn't season the food before it's cooked. You may need to salt your food and feel free to do so. Dearly will understand." Rayburn didn't start eating until Zack had passed the salt and pepper shakers to Camille and she had sprinkled the seasonings onto her food. She took a tentative bite, looked across at the anxious older man, and smiled.

"It's delicious, Mr. Prescott. You needn't worry about me losing any weight while I'm here." She laughed. "Indeed, if all the meals are this bountiful, I'll probably gain some."

"You could use some," Zack muttered under his breath for the benefit of her ears alone. She glared at him, but he seemed impervious to her.

Ever the gentleman, Rayburn drew her into amiable conversation, asking her questions about her life in Atlanta, her family, and her interests.

Zack was surly and uncommunicative and spoke only when asked a direct question by his father. If Rayburn noticed his son's sullenness, he didn't remark on it.

"Do you ski?" The question was asked so unexpectedly and out of context that Rayburn and Camille turned to Zack in bewilderment. Obviously the question had been directed toward her, and, to cover her alarm, Camille answered brightly, "Yes. A friend of mine has a boat and we go out whenever we can."

"Now, I meant snow ski," Zack persisted. Why was he talking about that sensitive subject when she was powerless to counteract him without revealing their antagonistic relationship to Rayburn?

"I went skiing a couple of years ago," she replied noncommittally.

"Surely you've *skied* since then. I would imagine that you *ski* quite often." Camille glowered at him, seething inside. He had put such an inflection on the word "ski" that she knew he wasn't referring to the snow sport at all.

"No. I skied once. I didn't like it. And I wasn't . . . I wasn't very good at it." She had ground out the first two sentences through clenched teeth, then stammered the last two as she dropped her head and looked at her empty plate, refusing to meet the mockery in his eyes.

"Oh, I don't know," he drawled. "You have

the . . . build . . . for it. I'd bet with practice you could become quite adept."

She shuddered in humiliation and rose abruptly from the table. "If . . . if you'll excuse me, Mr. Prescott. I . . . I'll be back shortly for our tour of the house." She practically ran from the room and as she left she heard Rayburn ask, "Did I miss something, Zachary? Why did she become so upset?"

Camille didn't wait to hear Zack's reply, but went through the house and across the terrace to the dowager house.

She bathed her face with cold water, muttering epithets pertaining to Zack's personality. Was he going to constantly torment her for the next several months that she would be here? Was there to be no escaping his sharp barbs about what had happened between them almost two years ago? How could she bear these continual reminders of a shameful mistake and an episode of her life she wished to be forever forgotten? She hated Zack Prescott!

And with that hate came a resolve not to submit to his cruelty. Just as her mother had always told her in her youth to ignore obnoxious boys who pestered her at school, she would ignore Zack's attempts to humiliate and embarrass her. When he realized that he couldn't reduce her to tears of shame, his sport would be spoiled and he would stop trying.

She felt restored as she went back into the

house. Rayburn was alone in the parlor. She didn't ask, but he informed her that Zack had gone out for the rest of the evening. She breathed a prayer of thanksgiving, but was faintly disappointed that he wasn't here to see her exhibition of courage and resolution.

Rayburn began his tour of the mansion in the double parlor. The two rooms were divided by heavy wooden sliding doors. One room was used as a living room while the other's main piece of furniture was a grand piano. Rayburn explained that Alice had played very well and was delighted to learn that Camille could play. He wanted the piano to stay.

Camille took notes as they strolled through the house, jotting down the pieces of furniture that she felt needed to be refinished, reupholstered, or removed completely. She wrote down the number of windows in each room, visualized how to achieve the greatest amount of floor space by moving a particular piece of furniture, and considered colors for each room that would blend harmoniously. She would peruse her sample books later tonight for more ideas. She noted that all the heavy sample and swatch books had been carried into the hallway. At least Zack wasn't totally lacking in manners.

They crossed the foyer, and Rayburn led her into the dining room where they had eaten dinner and which she had already appraised with a clinical eye. He showed her a smaller breakfast room and, finally, the kitchen, which she was happy to see was already equipped with modern plumbing and appliances. The changes in here would only be cosmetic and not structural. Dearly was still cleaning up after dinner and was thrilled when Camille asked her opinion on different color schemes. They discussed several, and Camille could tell by the housekeeper's enthusiasm that she had made a friend.

Rayburn and Camille walked up the broad staircase that graced one side of the wide hallway and curved its way up to the second floor. The oak banister was lovely, but needed to be rubbed to its original satin finish. That was going to require some elbow work, Camille noted.

Upstairs, Rayburn showed her through the rooms opening off the central hall. Camille planned to decorate it with the same detail as a room. There were four bedrooms, Rayburn explained. Two of them were connected by a bathroom, forming the master suite. Zack made one of these his bedroom.

"For the time being, we'll let Zack worry about his own decor," he said absently, and Camille sighed in relief.

Rayburn had moved out of the master suite after Alice's death and taken over a spacious bedroom across the hall. It boasted a rosewood tester bed, armoire, and dresser. Camille clapped her hands in delight over the beautiful antique furniture. Rayburn grinned like a young boy at her excitement.

"I had hoped the other bedroom would be a nursery," he sighed. "We'll leave that room as it is for the time being, although I wouldn't be opposed to your changing the wallpaper or anything else you saw fit to do in there. In the attic we've stored several area rugs, furniture, and bric-a-brac. You're free to browse through it and use anything you find."

Camille promised herself that one day soon she would scout out those possibilities.

"Dearly and Simon have their apartment over the garage and assure me that they are satisfied with it as it is. You might be able to convince them that a new coat of paint wouldn't hurt. Then when you've gained access, give it a good refurbishing," he chuckled.

Camille noticed that Rayburn seemed to be fatigued. The tour had taken longer than she thought it would, and it was getting late. Sparing his pride, she faked a broad yawn and affected embarrassment over it. "I'm sorry, but I think the day has been more taxing than I had realized. I think I'll go to bed now if you don't mind."

"Of course, of course," he agreed hastily.

As they went down the stairs, she explained the procedure she would follow. "In the morning we'll start looking through sample books and deciding

on the basic changes you want made. When we
have made all our choices, I'll call my studio and
they'll order everything from there. While we're
waiting for the materials to come in, we can start
doing some of the less glamorous jobs like sanding
floors, painting, regrouting tiles, etcetera. I may
need to hire some outside help for the heavier jobs.
Will that be all right?"

"Anything you need, my dear, don't hesitate to
ask for." He had escorted her to the back of the
house, but she stopped him from seeing her any
farther.

"I can go the rest of the way alone, Mr.
Prescott. I'll see you in the morning. Rest well."

"You too, Camille. If you need anything, pick
up the telephone extention and buzz Simon or
Dearly. All of the buttons for each extention are
well marked on the telephone."

"Thank you. Good night."

"Good night." He paused before he added shyly,
"I'm glad you're here, Camille. I think you'll be
good for all of us."

She turned and smiled, but, in her heart, she
really didn't agree with him. How could anything
good come out of her being here under the same
roof with a man whom she hated with reciprocated
intensity?

She walked through the shadows to her room.

A soft breeze was stirring the sheer curtains at

Camille's window when she opened her eyes a fraction and realized that it was still very early. She had drawn down the shades while she was undressing the night before, but after she had turned out the light and climbed into the four-poster bed, she discovered that with the windows obscured, the room became stifling. She got up, pulled the shades open, and crept across the darkened room back to bed. The drone of the overhead fan's motor and the cooling breeze soon lulled her to sleep despite her disturbing thoughts.

Now, she pushed back the sheet and tugged the tail of her nightshirt down over her bikini panties as she stumbled into the bathroom. She used the commode and was leaning over the sink, filling a glass with water, when she saw the snake coiled up behind the fixture.

Camille's scream ripped the air, and she dropped the glass in the sink, shattering it into a thousand pieces against the porcelain. She stood frozen for an instant and then jumped quickly into the bathtub. A snake couldn't get in there, could it? She screamed again when the long, striped snake began to uncoil. Over her whimpering she heard the front door open and then slam shut as heavy footsteps hurried in.

"Camille? Camille, are you all right?" Zack's anxious voice barely penetrated her terrified mind as she stared in fixed horror at the snake.

Zack's large frame filled the doorjamb. He was

dressed for the plantation in faded work jeans and a blue chambray shirt. His straw cowboy hat was pushed back on his head and a pair of leather gloves was sticking out of his belt.

He looked at Camille's white face as she stood cowering in the bathtub, not even aware of the fetching picture she made. Camille was too distraught to notice that he took in every detail of her figure. The pink nightshirt was cut like a man's dress shirt and just brushed the tops of her thighs. Her dark curls were in a tumbled tangle around her head.

"What in the hell is the matter with you?" he asked. He glanced quickly into the sink and seeing the broken glass asked, "Did you cut yourself?"

Camille pointed a shaking finger at the snake that had recoiled itself under the pedestal sink. "Snake," she croaked hoarsely.

Zack leaned down and spotted the object of her terror. In disgust mingled with a touch of humor he swore, "Oh, for God's sake."

Camille watched with disbelieving eyes as he grasped the snake behind its head and lifted its writhing body off the floor. Zack looked at the snake and then at her, shook his head in consternation, and walked out of the room. Camille heard the door slam again. He was gone and the snake with him, but still she stood trembling in the middle of the bathtub.

No more than a few minutes could have passed

before she heard her door open again and Zack returned to the bathroom. He stood there with his hands on his hips and stared at her scornfully.

"You scared the hell out of me when you screamed like that. Have you ever heard the story about the little boy who cried wolf?"

"He . . . he wasn't . . . poisonous?" She could barely control her stuttering tongue and quivering lips.

"Hardly. He's a friend of the family and lives in Dad's garden. He's a harmless garter snake."

She was infuriated by his calm explanation. It didn't matter to her what kind of snake it was. One species was as loathsome as another. She cried out defensively, "It could have been a water moccasin for all I knew."

"A *water* moccasin is usually found near the *water* and is ugly, the color of mud. They don't have the pretty stripes that our garter snake friends do." He was mocking her in a sing-song voice like a kindergarten teacher would use on children, and she couldn't take that mockery with her nerves already shattered as they were. Try though she did to hold them back, the tears came. Her shoulders shook and she stammered as she tried to speak. "I . . . I hate snakes. . . . I don't care what kind they are. . . . They . . . it frightened me. I couldn't . . . I couldn't . . ."

Then his arms were around her and he lifted her out of the tub. With one arm under her knees and the other supporting her shoulders, he carried her out of the bathroom and sat down on the bed, cradling her gently in his lap.

"You really were afraid, weren't you?" he whispered, brushing back strands of hair from her cheek. "I'm sorry I made fun of you. Shhh, he's gone. Everything is okay."

She turned her face into his chest and buried it in the soft fabric of his shirt as she once again started sobbing uncontrollably. He patted her back and stroked her cheek, repeating words of comfort. Finally, she was spent; her tears ran dry. She shuddered when she thought of the fool he must imagine her to be. Slowly she raised her head and looked at him apologetically. "I'm sorry I've held you up. You must have been getting an early start for the plantation. I'm glad you were up and about or I might still be standing in the bathtub." She smiled tremulously and looked away from his piercing blue eyes. "How do you suppose the . . . the snake got in?"

He laughed. "He probably heard all the talk about our charming houseguest and wanted to look you over. I imagine he came in through the plumbing somehow. Don't worry about it. I'll have Simon check to make sure everything is secured. I don't think you'll have another visit. You scared him as much as he scared you." She shuddered against him involuntarily.

His strong fingers reached out and tilted her

chin so that she was forced to look at him. "You've gotten my shirt all wet," he teased. She looked at the damp material where she had shed most of her tears.

"I'm sorry about that, too," she said softly and brushed her fingers across the cloth covering his hard chest. His body shook slightly, and she looked up to see a new light in his eyes. Camille was suddenly aware of their intimacy. She felt the soft denim of his jeans under her bare thighs and knew he could feel her heart pounding under the breast that was pressed against his broad chest.

Strong, sun-tanned fingers cupped the back of her head as he lowered his lips to hers. His kiss was firm and warm and chaste . . . at first. Then the all too vividly remembered sensuality of his mouth became real again. Camille's lips opened under the gentle pressure of his tongue and her breath caught in her throat when it explored her mouth with increasing fervor.

When they had to breathe, he pulled his lips from hers, but they didn't leave her face. He rained light kisses over her cheeks and forehead then trailed down her temple to give ardent attention to her ear. She sighed against his neck as she breathed in the fresh fragrance of his cologne. Who but Zack would apply cologne before going off to work in the fields all day?

Her sigh brought him back to her lips, and he teased them with soft, sipping kisses. Camille groaned as he lifted her arms and moved them around his neck while he firmly fastened his mouth on hers. The kiss was deep and thorough and arrested all Camille's senses. She was only vaguely aware of his hand moving to the top buttons of her nightshirt and the cool air against her bare skin. But she gasped and pulled her mouth away from his when she felt his hand slip into her opened nightshirt and cover her breast.

"Zack . . . please . . ." she breathed. His mouth had moved down her neck to the base of her throat, where he traced that small triangle with his tongue.

"Please what? What, Camille?" he asked huskily against her throat as his fingers coaxed a physical response from her breast.

"No, Zack, please—"

Whatever she was going to say was cut off abruptly as they heard a door slam. Simon's voice carried across the terrace as he chatted with Dearly while they made their way to the main house to start their morning chores.

Camille jumped off of Zack's lap and snatched together the front of her nightshirt. Shame and embarrassment bathed her cheeks with color as she faced him after securing the buttons down her front. She wished the night garment were longer. She was well aware that her long legs were completely bare and Zack took advantage of that fact as his eyes made a slow tour up and down her body.

A mocking grin lifted the corners of his mouth as he drawled, "What are you afraid of? Losing your virtue?"

She glared back at him and raised her chin haughtily. "That's a ludicrous question coming from *you!*"

He rose from the bed with the ease of a stretching jungle cat and pulled the cowboy hat low over his sun-bleached brows. He took a few steps forward, and only stubborn determination kept Camille rooted to her spot, for her inclination was to turn away from the blue eyes that burned her skin with their audacious, raking appraisal.

He stopped a few inches in front of her and murmured, "You're beautiful in the morning." He tugged playfully on one of her unruly curls and chucked her under the chin before he turned and walked out the screened door. He was whistling as he crossed the terrace. Whistling! It was that nonchalance that made her seethe with anger. He was so casual about what had just happened between them while her nerve endings were erupting like tiny volcanoes and filling her veins with a frightening fire.

Four

That morning Camille and Rayburn began the restoration of Bridal Wreath, discussing different colors, fabrics, and motifs. Camille was surprised at the older man's exquisite taste and pleased that they shared comparable visions of how the house should look when the redecorating was completed. Camille's own taste ran toward clean, simple, and graceful lines, lightly touched with elegance. She hated entering a room and feeling suffocated by the decor rather than being able to enjoy the room for its own merits. Rayburn seemed to approve of the wall colors, drapery samples, upholstery fabrics, and accent colors that she had tentatively selected. They tried several different combinations in each room until they agreed on the best ones, making certain that all the rooms would blend together. She took careful note of the order numbers stamped onto the backs of the various samples. When she ordered the materials, she wanted there to be no margin for error.

They continued with their work after lunch but, at Simon's suggestion, stopped in the middle of the afternoon. Simon had urged Camille to go to the dowager house and rest, but she knew that he was thinking about Rayburn's health and wanted the elder Prescott to lie down until dinner.

As far as the younger Prescott was concerned, Camille didn't see him until dinner. Throughout the day, she caught herself reliving the events of the morning, and was furious with herself for allowing him to kiss her with such unrestrained passion. He must have been laughing at her all day, knowing how she had practically fallen into his arms and succumbed to his expert caresses. Camille felt a stab of jealousy wondering on whom he had learned to be so knowledgeable in the art of loving.

She hated herself for being so pliable. He had barely touched her and yet she responded wantonly. The two years since Snow Bird seemed to dissolve, and his kisses brought back all the rapture she had felt when she lay in the security and warmth of his arms. His lips had tenderly demanded a response from hers and they had not been disappointed. His hands moved over her with a gentle familiarity that left her breathless. She had never allowed any other man such access to her body. Why Zack? What kind of power did he practice on her? All sense of propriety and moral conviction faded into oblivion when he held her in his arms. That was a dangerous situation. She had surrendered herself to his compromising persuasion once, and she still carried the guilt of that with her. She didn't intend to make that same mistake a second time.

Camille wore a simple cotton dress for dinner. It was a gold color that matched the golden flecks in her eyes. When she entered the parlor, Rayburn was sitting in a comfortable club chair that was destined to be reupholstered. It was one of his favorite chairs, and he had shyly asked Camille if he would be allowed to keep it. Laughing, she had agreed. Zack was standing at a long sideboard pouring himself a drink.

The navy slacks fit his long, muscular legs to perfection, and the ecru silk shirt caressed the sleek muscles of his back and shoulders every time he moved. He turned when he heard her enter and Camille saw that the silk didn't fully conceal the mat of tawny hair that covered his chest. She swallowed the annoying lump in her throat and murmured a low, "Good evening."

"Hello, Camille. Would you like a drink?" Even his voice was seductive.

"White wine, please. On the rocks."

"A real lady's drink, Camille," Rayburn approved. "I dislike women who drink hard liquor. I was just telling Zack about some of the plans we made today. You've reconfirmed my trust in your talents."

"Thank you for the compliment, Mr. Prescott. I hope that your son will be pleased with the results." She turned her eyes toward Zack, who was still standing after having crossed the room to hand her her drink. "If you should want to see the samples we've selected, I'll be glad to show them to you before I phone in my orders."

"Very kind of you, Camille, but I, too, will trust your judgment. I gave you my opinion on what I *don't* want the house to look like. Dad guarantees that you like simplicity in design. I'll leave the redecorating to the two of you and let the outcome be a surprise to me."

He was certainly in an amiable mood. She had expected him to be sarcastic and rude, especially after the scene in her room this morning. This Zack was more like the charmer who had first wooed her in Snow Bird. He was even more dangerous this way. She needed to be on her guard.

Over dinner, Rayburn urged his son to tell Camille about their plantation. She was impressed with the facts she finally coaxed out of a reticent Zack. He seemed almost embarrassed by the amount of property he owned and controlled and the amount of revenue it made him each year. Their main crop, of course, was cotton, but they also grew smaller quantities of other crops and even bred a few horses, an occupation that Zack wanted to develop more.

"Natchez has such a colorful history," Camille commented at a pause in the conversation. "I've always enjoyed reading books about it."

"It's interesting that most of the founding fathers chose to live on the high bluffs overlooking the Mississippi River and have their plantations on the other side in Louisiana. I guess they might have been the first Americans to commute to work." Zack smiled and his whole face lit up, the candles on the table reflected in the azure depths of his eyes. Camille was happy and at ease for the first time since her arrival.

"Some day soon, before the weather prevents an outing, I want you to take Camille over to the plantation and give her the deluxe tour," Rayburn said.

Camille met Zack's eyes across the table and her heart lurched at the idea of spending a day alone with him. His eyes dared her to look away from him as he held his stare, which carried a world of meaning for them. "I'd like to do that," he agreed as he pushed away from the table. "Right now, however, you'll have to excuse me. I have a date tonight."

His offhand, casual announcement hit Camille like a thunderbolt and she was immediately angry with herself for her reaction. So what if he was meeting a woman for the evening? It didn't matter to her in the least. Why then did the light mood of just moments ago fade as he said good night first to his father and then to her and with quick, light steps leave the room? His final glance at her had been mocking and arrogant, and her self-directed anger was transferred to him. She would show him that she couldn't care less if he had a dozen dates a night!

She agreed to a bridge game. Rayburn acted as her partner playing opposite the team of Simon and Dearly. She bantered with them and, on the outside, gave every impression of enjoying herself. On the inside, she was miserable, wondering who held Zack's attention for the long evening.

The days passed swiftly. Rayburn and Camille, after about a week of decision making, had chosen all the decorating materials that needed to be ordered. Camille made the telephone call to her assistant in Atlanta and meticulously went over the order with her employee, who would do the actual ordering. Camille urged her to call if anything wasn't available or if there was any trouble at all over the order, then asked to speak to her mother. They talked a short while, Camille assuring her only parent that she was well and that the Prescotts were charming. *The older one anyway,* she added under her breath.

She rarely saw Zack during the daytime. He left for the plantation early and returned just before dinner. Many nights he was absent from the evening meal and Rayburn would comment that he had made other plans. His absence was sorely felt, for as much as Camille hated to admit it, he was the center of her thoughts these days, and she enjoyed having him across the table from her in the evenings. Even though he sometimes spoke in suggestive, reminiscent double entendres that only she understood, she liked his company. His arrogance and sarcasm hurt her deeply, but she favored suffering them over not seeing him at all.

He never mentioned the woman he dated, and Camille would never have learned about her except for Rayburn's referring to "the widow Hazelett." Camille tried to continue her dinner calmly when he made his first reference to Zack's female interest on a night when Zack was out.

"The widow Hazelett?" asked Camille with affected disinterest.

"Yes. Zack sees her often, though I heartily disapprove of the woman. She's . . . artificial, phony. Every time she's around Zack she watches over him like a mother bear with her cub, almost daring anyone else to come near him. She has newfangled ideas about raising children, too. She has two of her own. They're cute kids, polite and smart. But she hustles them off to boarding school every fall and then fills their summers with camp and trips to their grandparents. I hope Zack has more sense than to link up with the likes of *her*."

Camille smiled to herself although she kept a straight face for Rayburn's benefit. At least she had some idea of the company Zack was keeping, and his father didn't approve of the woman. That was one thing in Camille's favor.

Suddenly she drew herself upright. What did she care abut Zack's love life? She didn't want him, that was for sure! What kind of man would seduce an innocent girl and then feel no guilt or remorse for having stolen from her what didn't belong to him unless he was her husband? No! She didn't want a man like Zachary Prescott.

She almost convinced herself.

With the help of the local Yellow Pages, Camille began consulting with carpenters, painters, paperhangers, furniture upholsterers and refinishers, and seamstresses. The name Prescott was well known, as was Bridal Wreath. She was glad to learn that she would have no trouble finding artisans to help with the restoration of the house.

The days fell into a comfortable unhurried routine. Camille began to notice that the fall season was upon them. The seasonal flowers on the terrace had ceased their profuse blooming except for the chrysanthemums, which provided Bridal Wreath with a rainbow of autumn colors.

One morning the low clouds that had shrouded the landscape for several days opened up, and it began to rain. Simon called Camille's room to tell her that Rayburn wouldn't be down for breakfast and that she was to take the day off. He told her that the old gentleman had decided to spend the day in his room going over the plantation's accounting books. Camille knew that Zack handled all of the business for their farm, but she was warmed by the fact that he still made his father feel important enough to have access to the ledgers.

She decided, as she dressed in a pair of comfortable jeans and a dark gingham shirt, that she would spend this rainy day going through the attic. She had wanted to investigate what treasures it might hold ever since Rayburn mentioned it to her.

As she stared out across the torrential rainfall making a lake out of the terrace, she realized with dismay that she didn't have an umbrella. She went into the bathroom and draped a thick terry towel over her head. She had pulled her hair back into a ponytail and secured it with a large barrette.

She stepped hesitantly onto the covered porch of the dowager house, took a long breath, ducked her head, and ran pell-mell across the slippery terrace.

She collided with a tall, broad barrier of muscle and recognized Zack's low, deep laugh as his arm went around her waist.

"Hey, watch out or you'll fall down. Under here." She peered at him from under the towel and saw that he was holding a huge umbrella over them both. With his arm still supporting her, they maneuvered their way around rapidly forming puddles to the back door of the house.

When they entered, Zack shook out the umbrella and leaned it against the wall, running his fingers through dampened sun-streaked hair. "Boy, what a downpour. Simon realized that you had no umbrella, so I was on my way to fetch you. You should have waited for me." His smile was bright and Camille's heart hadn't stopped pounding from the close contact she had just had with his vibrant body. His jeans were old, comfortable-looking, and tight, hugging his hips as he swaggered through the doorway leading into the kitchen.

"Come on. The bisquits are in the oven. How do you like your eggs?"

"You're cooking breakfast?" Camille asked incredulously.

"Sure," he shrugged. "Why not? I'm not helpless." He sounded indignant. "How do you like your eggs?" he repeated with distinct enunciation on each word.

"Scrambled," she answered with a smile and crossed to the counter to pour a cup of coffee from the coffeemaker plugged into the wall.

He turned toward the stove and asked over his shoulder, "Firm or soft?"

"Firm," she replied. "Very." He scowled, lowering his thick eyebrows in mock distaste as he looked at her.

"I'll take mine out first," he growled as he

began breaking eggs into a bowl. "I'm sorry there will be no grits this morning. Every time I try to cook them, I let them cook too dry and they get gummy. Then Dearly scolds me when she has to clean the pan." Camille laughed.

The aroma of fried bacon and baking bisquits filled the kitchen as Camille set the table for them. Zack explained that Dearly had gone to visit a sick friend, and Simon was upstairs with Rayburn. The silence in the house along with the heavy rain outside encapsulated them in a private world, and Camille smiled as she imagined that this was what it would be like if they had met under different circumstances and fallen in love and married. They could have shared many mornings like this. There may have even been a baby by now. She wasn't aware of the revealing, tender expression on her face as she stared at Zack's back until he turned from the range holding a plateful of fluffy eggs and caught her at her musings.

He grinned wickedly as he set the platter down on the small table and threw his leg over the back of the chair and sat down. "I don't know what the fantasy is, but I wish to hell I was in on it. It looks damned pleasant."

Camille made a big production of buttering her featherlight bisquit and wouldn't meet his eyes. "I . . . uh . . . I was just anticipating what I'll find in the attic today."

"Liar," he whispered softly. The intimacy in his

voice made her fingers tremble, and she dropped her knife onto her plate with a loud clatter.

They ate in silence for a few minutes and Camille complimented him on his cooking. When she was finished and began gathering up the plate and cutlery, he surprised her by saying, "I'll do the dishes. I need another cup of coffee anyway. Have a good day in the attic."

She left the warm ambience of the kitchen while Zack still sat at the table, absently sipping on a cup of scalding coffee.

The entrance to the attic was in the room that Rayburn referred to with stubborn optimism as the nursery. Camille stopped in front of his door and knocked timidly. Simon answered and Camille warned that she would be overhead and for them not to worry if they heard thumping and bumping. Rayburn called out a "good morning" from across the room. Simon shut the door as Camille went into the other room.

The stairs leading to the attic were in a closet. Camille bravely climbed them, brushing spider webs aside as she encountered them. She opened the attic door and reached for the light switch where Simon had told her she would find it. She located it by feel, for the attic had no windows and the darkness in front of her was complete. At a flick of her wrist, the attic was bathed with light from a naked bulb suspended on a dangling cord.

The room, for that was what it was, ran almost

the length of the house. Trunks and luggage were stacked against one wall under the eaves, and boxes of every size were scattered with some semblance of order around the room. Shelves lined one wall, and they were loaded with packing crates, most of them labeled with an inventory of their contents. Most of the furniture was shrouded with dust sheets, and Camille could only guess at what was underneath the covers. Apparently, this was going to be quite a chore.

Impatiently brushing back a few strands of hair curling around her cheek, she got to work. After reaching for several boxes on the lower shelves, her blouse came out of the waistband of her jeans. She tied the ends of it in a knot across her stomach.

The first few boxes she opened contained bric-a-brac that was not all that impressive, and she didn't discover any hidden treasures. She did find some crystal bowls that could be used in the dining room once they were washed and sparkling again. She sat that box aside.

As she reached for another, she noticed that the storm outside had intensified. Rain pounded on the roof directly over her head, and there was a crash of thunder nearby. She was reaching for a box on one of the higher shelves when a voice behind her commanded that she not try it.

"You might hurt yourself. I'll get it for you," Zack offered as he crossed the floor.

"You scared me!" she cried, wondering how he had climbed the stairs without her hearing him and then remembered the loud commotion of the storm. She didn't want him to know how keenly his appearance affected her. "Why did you sneak up on me like that? And I can get the box myself!" she declared stubbornly and turned to reach for the box again. She raised her arms over her head and her fingers just touched the edge of the shelf when she felt Zack's hard chest press into her back. He leaned forward and his strong hands reached beyond hers toward the box. Instead of grasping it, as she expected him to do, his hands closed over hers, imprisoning her in his arms. With her arms raised as they were, and him so uncomfortably close against her back, it was a very vulnerable position she found herself in. She was just about to tell him what she thought of his superior attitude when a loud crack of lightning striking nearby split the atmosphere, and the attic was plunged into complete darkness as the electric light went out.

Camille stifled a small scream.

"It's okay. Everything's fine. There's no need to panic. I'm here with you."

Zack's voice was calm, but Camille wanted to laugh at his reassuring words. Little did he know that she would not have been nearly so frightened had he *not* been here with her. It was his over-whelming, masculine presence behind her in the darkness that frightened her so.

The large brown hands covering hers relieved their pressure somewhat but began a slow stroking motion up her arms to her shoulders. He massaged them for a moment, concentrating on the base of her neck, then moved his hands tantalizingly down her sides before clasping them around her and resting them on her bare stomach.

The breath stirring Camille's hair was ragged, and the lips planting small kisses on the nape of her neck were compelling. One hand flattened against her stomach while the other slipped into the waistband of her jeans where his thumb caressed her navel with a hypnotizing laziness.

"Camille," he groaned as he untied the knot holding her shirt tight under her breasts. His mouth moved from her ear to her cheek and kissed the corner of her mouth while breathing her name. Camille, with a tickling sensation fluttering in the lower part of her body, turned toward him, softly calling his name. Of their own volition, her arms went around his neck, bringing his face down to hers as their lips sought each other in the darkness.

Their bodies moved together as his mouth fastened on hers. She matched his ardor, tasting him, smelling the unique scent that was Zack, feeling the silkiness of his burnished hair as she clenched her fingers in it.

He slipped one hand to her hips and drew her closer, forcing her to recognize the power of his desire. She trembled as she realized that hers was just as great.

He reached behind his neck and captured one of her hands. Camille felt his tongue in her palm and the warm breath on her wrist before he placed her hand against his chest and hoarsely insisted, "Touch me, Camille."

She hesitated only a moment before she lay her head against his chest while she unbuttoned two buttons on his shirt and slipped her hand inside. Her fingers danced lightly over the mat of hair and then, as she became more confident, explored the hardness of the muscles underneath.

"Oh, God," he moaned before his mouth once more sought hers and lowered onto it.

His hands slid under her shirt and fumbled with the clasp on the front of her bra.

The light came back on.

They jumped guiltily away from each other and blinked against the suddenly harsh light as if trying to remember where they were and what they had been doing before being swept away by their passion.

Camille risked looking at Zack, but he was running his hands through his hair in such agitation and frustration that she dared not speak. She turned her back on him and straightened her clothing, tucking her shirt chastely back into her waistband.

"Zack, are you and Camille all right up there?" Simon's voice came from the bottom of the stairs.

Zack laughed mirthlessly and called back bitterly, "Yes, we're fine. The lights are back on."

"Okay, I was just checking." They heard Simon's footsteps recede back into the room below and again there was silence in the attic except for their labored breathing and the rain overhead.

Camille shyly raised her eyes to meet Zack's sneer. "Congratulations, Camille. You have been saved from another of my ravishings." She was hurt by the coldness in his voice, but she didn't speak as he turned toward the descending staircase. He paused and looked toward her. "This time," he said before his head disappeared beyond the first steps.

Five

That evening at dinner Camille learned that Zack had gone to Kentucky for a few days to look at a stud farm and talk to a hose breeder who had enjoyed great success in the field.

Rayburn told her, "I tried to dissuade him from going in this weather, but he was adamant. He can be very mule-headed sometimes." The older man smiled at her. "I guess he feels like he couldn't do much at the plantation with these heavy rains. Did you have any luck in the attic?" he asked.

Camille tried to hide the abashment any reminder of that morning in the attic brought to mind. She winced as she remembered Zack's departing scornful expression and harsh words, but she collected herself and answered as excitedly as she could. "Yes. I found some crystal that I think will look lovely on the sideboards here in the dining room. A chaise longue could be used in one of the bedrooms if it were recovered and refinished.

There was a tea table that I think will go nicely in the parlor. Some of the other things I found, I'm reserving judgment on." She picked at her food and really wasn't interested in the conversation, though manners drilled into her by Martha Jameson forbade her showing it.

Rayburn was apparently aware of her mood, for he asked solicitously, "Do you not feel well, Camille?"

"Oh, I'm sorry, Mr. Prescott. You must forgive my moodiness. I think that the rainy day has gotten to me, and I'm homesick," she lied convincingly. He seemed satisfied with her answer, though when she looked up at him, his blue eyes, which weren't as startling a hue as Zack's, were piercing her with a shrewd stare. Did he know more about what was going on around him than he let on?

He reached across the table and patted her hand. "Camille, I understand that and hope the mood will pass quickly. Is there anything I can do?"

His kindness and sincerity were too much for her shattered emotions, and, to her horror, she burst into tears.

"I'm sorry," she apologized as she rose from the table. "I think I'll go to the dowager house and go to bed." Before he could reply, she fled from the room.

She spent a restless night, tossing and turning and waiting for elusive sleep. But when sleep finally came, she had disturbing dreams of Zack.

How could one man be so tender and loving one moment and so bitter and hateful the next? How could he reduce her to a powerless chattel in his arms and then act as if it had been her idea, her fault? His being gone for these next few days was a blessing. Why then was she so abysmally unhappy to know that he wasn't around?

He haunted her. He tormented her. It wasn't fair! He had been in the background of her mind for the past two years, and now he was in the forefront, and the constant reminder of their affair in Snow Bird was torturous. Why did he kiss her so ardently when he felt such strong contempt for her? She was a fool to stay and subject herself to this mental cruelty. But with characteristic candor, she asked herself if it wouldn't be worse to leave now and never see Zack Prescott again. Truthfully, she admitted that it would.

With a long shuddering sigh, she fell into an exhausted sleep.

When she saw Rayburn the next morning, he didn't comment on the dark circles under her eyes or her pale cheeks. She apologized for her juvenile behavior the night before and tried to laugh it off, but knew for certain that the sensitive old man could see through her ruse.

Immediately after breakfast, she started to work on the banister. After a dark residue, left by years of palms being dragged down it, had been lightly scraped away, it needed to be polished to its former patina. It was a messy job and required hours of long, tedious work. *Just what I need,* thought Camille, *to get my mind off my problems.* She tackled the chore wearing her oldest pair of jeans, her hair tied back with a scarf.

The banister took two full days of effort to complete to her satisfaction, but despite Rayburn's urgings to get some help for it, she refused his offer and chose to do it all herself.

After work on the banister was finished, and its wood shone with a warm glow, she started working on the floors. Even though most of the floor space in each room would be covered by heirloom area rugs, Camille felt that the wood beneath them needed to be sanded and revarnished. She had contracted the O'Malleys, a father and son team, to do this atrocious, seemingly overwhelming task.

When the O'Malleys arrived for the first day's work, Camille was immediately pleased with them and glad that Rayburn had recommended them. For a man his age, Sean O'Malley moved with alacrity and proceeded to go about his work with the enthusiasm of a man half his age. Rick O'Malley was about Zack's age. His sandy hair and bright brown eyes, along with a ready smile and teasing manner, made him instantly likable. He flirted with Camille shamelessly, but in such an agreeable way, that she was helpless to resist it. She teased and flirted back, and the long hours of hard work, which she insisted on sharing, passed quickly over the next several days.

Though shorter than Zack, Rick had a muscularly compact body that worked with as much energy and agility as that of his father. He chatted easily with Dearly, Simon, and Rayburn whenever they came into the room in which he was working, but even after days of listening to his bantering, Camille realized that he rarely talked about himself. She noticed, too, that frequently there was a poignancy or sadness around his eyes that would momentarily overshadow his merry face. He was quick to hide it if he caught anyone watching him.

One afternoon as they were about to leave, she escorted them out to the front porch. Sean O'Malley walked toward their truck parked in the driveway, but Rick held back and somewhat shyly asked Camille if she would go out with him that Friday night.

"There's a high school football game this weekend. A big rivalry. The whole town turns out for this one. Would you like to go?"

She hesitated only an instant, thinking about Zack and how he would react. "Yes," she said eagerly. Why should she care what Zack thought about her having a date? She was an adult. He certainly had no claim on her, nor she on him.

"Good. I'll see you tomorrow." Rick bounced off the front porch, did a ridiculous jig on his way to the truck, and reduced Camille to a fit of giggles with his antics.

Friday afternoon found her on her hands and knees working in a corner of the parlor when Simon brought in a pitcher of cold lemonade.

Rick came over to her and pulled her to her feet. "Take a break why don't you, lady," he teased as he drew her up. "Look at that face! We're trying to stain the floor, not each other," he laughed, taking a handkerchief out of his pocket and wiping the stain from her face.

At that moment, when Camille was playfully dodging Rick's ministrations, Zack stepped under the arch that separated the parlor from the hallway. His face was stony, his eyes dark with a brewing storm of temper as he viewed the sight before him. The muscles in his jaw twitched with tension and Camille saw that he was clenching his fists at his sides as if forcing control over them.

"Hello, Zack." Her statement was simple enough, but it intentionally held a warning in it for the innocent Rick. He turned and saw Zack standing in a militant stance and looked back quickly toward Camille with a puzzled, quizzical expression on his face.

He recovered himself and crossed the room with his hand outstretched. "Zack, long time no see, you ol' son of a gun! Here I've been working in your house all week and haven't seen the lord of the manor yet. How are you?"

"Fine, Rick, how are you?" Zack's words were clipped as he shook hands with Rick. "I see your work here hasn't been too boring. If you'll excuse me." He nodded at Rick and Sean O'Malley, but ignored Camille. He turned abruptly toward the hall and bumped into Rayburn, who had witnessed the entire scene.

"Hello, son. How was your trip?"

"Beneficial, I think," Zack answered curtly.

"Good. We're glad to have you back."

"Really? It appears to me that my arrival may have put a pall over all the fun everyone seems to be having." With that he stalked upstairs. Rayburn followed his son's angry back with his eyes and then looked at Camille. She wished the floor on which she had been working so hard would suddenly open up and swallow her.

Then she was suffused with anger at Zack. Why should she feel ashamed? She hadn't done anything wrong, and even if she had, it was none of Zack Prescott's concern. She raised her chin and proclaimed, "I would think that a few days away from home would improve one's humor. It just goes to show how wrong one can be."

If she expected a censure from Rayburn, she was surprised when he threw back his head of white hair and laughed out loud.

Rick looked nervous and wiped his sweaty palms on his jean-clad thighs. He had known Zack Prescott since grade school and recognized that look in Zack's eyes. It meant trouble, and anyone with good sense steered clear of him when his blue eyes took on that particular glacial quality. "I'd better get back to work," he muttered, guiltily shifting his eyes away from Camille.

Before he left that day, Rick pulled Camille aside and whispered anxiously. "Listen, Camille, I didn't mean to trespass on someone else's territory. Are you and Zack . . . I mean, is there . . . ?"

Because he was finding it hard to put his question into words, Camille interrupted. "Rick, I'm looking forward to our date tonight. There is no reason for me not to go out with you."

He wiped a few beads of perspiration from his upper lip and sighed. "Well, I'm glad about that. I wouldn't want to make anyone mad at me." He laughed nervously then socked her playfully on the chin. "I'll see you around seven. Okay?"

She agreed and he left.

At their early dinner, Zack was sullen and uncommunicative, which was what Camille had expected, but Rayburn seemed bent on having a good time. He told Camille stories about his growing up. His adventures on the Mississippi River sounded every bit as colorful as those of Tom Sawyer and Huckleberry Finn. In spite of her annoyance over Zack's brooding mood, she laughed at the tall tales Rayburn was spinning. She noticed that the more she laughed, the more surly

Zack became. *Well, let him sulk,* she thought defiantly, and laughed even harder.

When the meal was finished, Rayburn leaned back in his chair expansively and wiped the tears of mirth from his eyes. "Yes, that summer of '12 was one to remember." He paused a moment before asking, "What time is Rick picking you up, Camille? Don't let us keep you. She's going to the football game with him tonight," he added in way of explanation to Zack. Camille glanced at him quickly, but he only shrugged indifferently and took a drink of his iced tea.

"About seven," she answered Rayburn, stung by Zack's apathy to his father's announcement.

"Well then, you'd better go get ready—not that you don't look beautiful now." He pushed his chair back and said, almost as an afterthought, "Zack, why don't you take Camille to the plantation tomorrow? She's worked hard this week, and I'd like for her to take the entire weekend off."

"I don't know—" she started, but Zack interrupted her.

"Okay. I didn't have anything else to do." He pushed back from the table. "I'll see you in the morning. Dress casually." Without another word, he stomped out of the dining room.

Of all the nerve! Camille screamed silently. She faced Rayburn and noticed that his white eyebrows were raised almost to his hairline in a nonverbal query as he studied the doorway recently vacated by his son.

Camille excused herself soon after that and went to the dowager house to dress for her date with Rick. More than ever she was determined to have a good time tonight. But she was torn between anticipation and dread for the next day.

Rick's effervescence was infectious, and a short time after he picked her up, Camille had almost forgotten Zack's brooding and his less-than-enthusiastic response to Rayburn's suggestion that they visit the plantation the following morning.

The evening was cool and clear and perfect for a football game. After parking his car in the stadium parking lot, Rick took Camille's arm and they walked for what seemed like miles over rocky, dusty ground toward the brightly lit, gaily decorated field. The bands representing each school vied for supremacy in volume, and they laughed together as they kept step first with the cadence, of one, then another until they were weak with the effort.

Camille wore a plaid wool kilt and matching sweater, but soon wished she had left her suede pumps at home and worn some lower-heeled, more comfortable walking shoes.

They located their seats just moments before the kick-off, and amidst the shouting and cheering, Rick introduced her to the other couples nearby. She didn't catch all of the names, but that didn't seem to be important. Everyone was soon caught up in the spirit of the game.

Rick, with exaggerated lasciviousness, ogled the jiggling cheerleaders cavorting in front of the stands. Camille and her date clapped their hands and stomped their feet, laughing like two teenagers. She felt more relaxed than she had for weeks and was enjoying herself immensely.

Then she saw Zack. He was climbing the steep stadium steps, his arm draped around the shoulders of a tall, slender woman with shining blond hair. Spectators in the stands shouted greetings to the handsome couple as they made their way to their seats, stopping nearly every other row to chat with someone. Zack's eyes, though he was joking and talking animatedly, scanned the crowd until they fell on Camille and Rick. Rick had been distracted by a man on his other side, so he didn't see when Zack's blue eyes lighted on Camille and gave her a mocking, insolent smile. She turned her head away quickly and tried to ignore him and his gorgeous date, the hard pounding of her heart, and the sudden streak of jealousy that coursed through her.

She was further discomfited when Zack and the woman finally sat down only two rows from her and Rick. *Why?* Now her whole evening would be ruined! It was frustrating to have to admit that, but she knew it to be true. For as much as she wanted to enjoy the football game and the laughing, affable Rick, she couldn't concentrate on anything but the back of Zack's head and the other one that moved too close to his far too often, trailing blond tresses across his shoulders. Was this the Hazelett woman that Rayburn had mentioned with such dislike?

At halftime, Rick plied her with tepid hot chocolate and stale popcorn. The fervor of the fans intensified during the exciting second half of the game. The score favored first one team, then the next. When, during the final minute of the game, the home team scored a touchdown, the fans went crazy. Everyone was on their feet, shouting, whistling, clapping their hands in rhythm to the fight song being blared out by the band. In his excitement, Rick hugged Camille tightly, lifting her off her feet and kissing her soundly on the mouth. She was laughing at his jostling enthusiasm when, over his broad shoulders, she locked gazes with Zack, who was staring at them over the frantic crowd. He stood perfectly still. All his mocking smiles were gone. His face was set and grim, carved out of granite. Only his eyes were alive. They flashed blue fire. He turned away from her scornfully. The spirit in the stadium reached obsessive proportions, and Camille was thankful that no one noticed her lack of exuberance.

Rick took her out for pizza before driving her back to Bridal Wreath. At the door of the dowager house, she thanked him for the good time and submitted when he took her upper arms in his hands and drew her to him for a dispassionate good-night kiss. As he pulled back, she recognized that sadness which she had noticed before on his strong, kind face. He stroked her cheek gently before wishing her good night and walking away. Was there a slump to his shoulders and a lethargy to his usually bouncing walk? *We all suffer our private torments, don't we?* she thought philosophically as she went into her room.

The morning's weather was a repetition of the evening before, crackling with the briskness of fall. Camille pulled on a pair of designer jeans that flattered her slender legs and hips. She wore a long-sleeved, beige shirt and tied the sleeves of a navy cardigan around her neck. She stepped into a pair of comfortable boots that had seen too many seasons, but were too comfortable to consider throwing away.

It was still early, but she crossed the terrace, walked through the screened back porch, and entered the kitchen, where Dearly was making bisquits and had already brewed a pot of coffee.

"Good morning, Camille. Did you sleep well? I hear you're going out for the day with Zack. Better watch yourself. He has the reputation of being a lady's man." She laughed merrily as she put the bisquits in the oven. Camille blanched as she remembered the blonde that clung so possessively to Zack at the football game. She turned quickly to pour herself a cup of coffee. "Yes, sir, he's a lady's man all right," Dearly continued. "With those blue eyes, what could you expect? I would get so aggravated when he was in high school. The girls would call here giggling and asking for Zack. Incessantly that telephone was ringing. And he liked the girls okay, but was much more interested in sports and cars then. While he was in college . . . well, I don't know too much about that because he was gone, but when he came back here to live, he had to fight off every debutante and her mother for miles around. There were several women that he dated off and on for years, but one by one they gave up on him and married someone else. He never seemed upset to lose one of those women to another man."

Camille didn't interrupt this revealing monologue and began setting the table while Dearly deftly sliced and sectioned grapefruits. "Then about two years ago, he went through a black period. Whew! He was so moody and cross all the time. He just withdrew into himself and wouldn't talk to anyone. He was constantly muttering deprecations about women in general, and we finally figured out that he had fallen for someone and she had done him dirty. Probably got tired of his stalling and up and married someone else. Of course, he never told us anything about it. We never knew who she was, but she hurt him."

Two years ago. So he was in Utah to get over an

affair that had gone awry. He was out to prove his masculinity and reestablish his self-esteem, and Camille had been his guinea pig. Mr. Zachary Prescott should have felt very good about himself after she had fallen like a ripe plum into his hands and put up next to no resistance when he had seduced her.

Dearly commanded her attention again. "He went for months without seeing any woman, then he started dating this Erica Hazelett, and, if you ask me, she isn't right for our Zack. Any woman that sends her kids off for months at a time so they won't interfere with her social calendar is no proper mother. And since Zack never had a mother, much less brothers and sisters, he's always said he wanted several children . . . *if* he ever got married." She sighed. "We've just about given up hope of there ever being babies in this house."

Camille absently buttered one of the bisquits, which by now were out of the oven and in a basket on the table. She sipped her coffee and sighed. Whoever she was who hurt Zack had wounded him deeply. Camille should know better than anyone how bitter his attitude toward the female sex was and how shamelessly he used them for his own selfish gratification. Did his contemptuous attitude stem from a desire for revenge on the whole sex for the deeds of one whom he had obviously loved?

The object of her musings sauntered into the

kitchen dressed in a pair of jeans and a matching jacket pulled on over a lightweight, white turtleneck sweater.

"Good morning, ladies," he said cheerfully and gave Dearly a smacking kiss on the cheek. Camille had expected him to be as sulky as he had been the night before at dinner. She was not prepared for this lighthearted, debonair man who crossed to the coffeemaker and poured himself a cup while humming "Oh, What a Beautiful Morning" under his breath. Her last impression of him had been the angry, cold statue staring at her scornfully while Rick held her in his strong arms. Didn't Zack even remember that disdainful way he had looked at her when he saw Rick kissing her?

"Ready to go?" he asked as he slid into the chair and grabbed a hot bisquit, juggling it between his hands until he dropped it onto his plate.

"Yes," she replied, too shocked by the metamorphosis of his personality to say anything else.

"Good. I've got a full schedule of activities planned for us. Hurry up and eat your breakfast."

"Yes, sir!" Camille said briskly and saluted him. The sparkle in his bright eyes made Camille's heart jump erratically. If only . . .

Zack helped her into the cab of a pickup that had seen many years and endless miles of country roads. The blue paint was faded and chipped, and one window had been broken but remained intact.

"If we were going on a real date, I would drive my car, but this is much more suited to a tour of the plantation. Do you mind too much?"

"No, not at all," Camille replied evenly, though her pulse was racing after that brief contact with him when his strong fingers had closed around her upper arm as he handed her into the truck. Would she never be immune to his touch?

Zack turned left out of Bridal Wreath's driveway and drove the short distance to the intersection with Highway 65. They headed west toward the river. Just before they drove onto the suspension bridge spanning it, Zack pointed to a house perched on a high bluff to their left. "That's The Briars. It offers a lovely view of the river and boasts that Jefferson Davis married Varina Howell in the parlor. The house was built around 1812."

Camille caught only a fleeting glimpse of the beautiful home and grounds as they drove past. She had leaned toward Zack to look out his side of the truck, and her breast accidentally brushed against his arm. A thrilling current shot through her body. She withdrew quickly and scooted to the far side of the cab, hoping that he had not been aware of the effect his touch had on her.

She feigned absorbing interest as they crossed the Mississippi River, but, indeed, it was a thrilling sight. Several barges that she knew were immense looked like toy boats on the vastness of the river. Camille sighted Natchez-Under-the-Hill, a historic part of the old city. Just as she was about to comment on it, Zack said, "One night we'll go to Under-the-Hill and have dinner. Cock of the Walk has the best fried catfish anywhere. Please don't tell Dearly I said so." His eyes locked with hers and they smiled at each other, his teeth white and gleaming. Why was he so devilishly handsome?

They reached the Louisiana side of the river in a matter of minutes and drove through the small community of Vidalia before continuing west. A few miles farther. Zack turned north into a road spanned by a metal arch. The words "Prescott Plantation" were spelled out with curving metal letters.

For Camille the rest of the morning passed in a kaleidoscope of impressions. Zack drove her over acres of fields, explaining the crops grown in each one, how they rotated them, when they knew to let one lie fallow, the specialized service performed by one piece of equipment or another. As they encountered employees working in various capacities, Zack slowed the pickup down to call out a greeting. He knew everyone by name, which was no small accomplishment. Camille was amazed to see how many workers it took to manage the multifaceted plantation.

Zack's pet interest was the stud farm he was trying to establish. He showed her his stables and the few horses he already owned. Some of them were ponies only a few months old that had been born in the spring. She commented on how attractive and healthy they appeared, though she knew virtually nothing about horseflesh. Zack admitted that it was a new field for him, too, but he was determined to learn about this lucrative enterprise.

Camille studied him as he spoke about his future plans for this and every aspect of the plantation. His voice became excited and eager. His face shone with anticipation at the goals he had set for himself, and Camille realized that Zack would always have a new horizon. He was not a man to reach a plateau in his life and stop there. He would look for another challenge. She had gained a new insight into his character.

It came to her quietly then that she loved him.

It was a bittersweet awakening. She longed to reach out and touch him, to share her discovery with him, but of course she couldn't. Didn't he feel the power of her love? Didn't he realize the tumult that was raging inside her? *Zack, I love you,* she cried silently.

He had taken off his felt cowboy hat, which had replaced the straw one in deference to the season, and his sun-burnished curls stirred in the cool autumn breeze. He was leaning against a fence, one booted foot on the bottom rail, his hands dangling casually over the top one. He was the essence of masculinity. From the first time she had seen him in Utah, Camille had recognized his virility and been intimidated by it. She confessed to herself now that it was Zack's encompassing appeal that had frightened her. When she ran from him . . . from his bed . . . had she realized then that this was a man whom she could love with an all-consuming passion? Had she fled, convincing herself that it was from shame and self-loathing, when actually it had been out of a fear of rejection? She remembered experiencing a rushing feeling of love as he had held her in the stillness of the night. *Love?* she had asked herself. *No! It doesn't happen this way.* But it had. She admitted it now. She had loved him from the first.

Zack turned his head and caught her intense perusal of him. Color flooded her cheeks. Could he read her mind? Did he know how much she loved him?

He brushed a stray curl from her forehead; his fingers seemed to brand her flesh. "I think your plantation is wonderful, Zack. I mean that."

"I know you do," he said seriously. Then in a lighter tone he asked if she were hungry.

"Yes!" she declared. "I'm starved."

He laughed. "Good, because I'm taking you to a very special place for lunch."

He ushered her back toward the truck, and, when they left the plantation property, they headed east toward Natchez.

As they drove through the city, Zack pointed out historic sites to Camille, who tried vainly to absorb them all. He was apparently well acquainted with the history of his hometown for he quoted facts like a professor. There were over two hundred antebellum buildings in Natchez, and each one had its own claim to fame. Such illustrious guests as Henry Clay, Aaron Burr, Lafayette, Andrew and Rachel Jackson, Mark Twain, and Stephen Foster were reputed to have visited with Natchez families and spent time in some of the lovely homes.

The restaurant Zack had chosen for lunch was the Post House in the old King's Tavern. Zack explained that it was the oldest building in Natchez, built before 1798. Indian runners delivered the first United States mail to the King's Tavern after the city came under United States jurisdiction that year. The site marked the end of the legendary Natchez Trace, which was a well-marked trail through the wilderness to Nashville, Tennessee. As they went through the doorway of the building, Zack pointed out the bullet holes still in the walls, remnants of an early Indian attack.

The restaurant was low-ceilinged and used pioneer memorabilia for is decor. Camille was enchanted. Not only was she here in this historic spot that had been the site of so many colorful events, but she was sharing it with Zachary Prescott; and if he had been a backwoodsman who had just traversed the treacherous Natchez Trace, he couldn't have been more intriguing to her.

With her permission he ordered for them. They had steaming bowls of seafood gumbo, baked chicken with cornbread dressing, and a variety of vegetables and relishes.

Covertly she watched him as they ate. He seemed to be relaxed and enjoying himself, though spending this day with her had been more or less an order from his father. He spoke to nearly every-one who came in, and introduced her to those who stopped by their table to chat.

They were lingering over cups of coffee when Camille commented, "Your father seems to be feeling better, doesn't he?"

"Yes. I think having you here and working on the house has lifted his spirits considerably. His health will never be what it was before the attack though, and I worry about it constantly."

"I'm sure you do, Zack." She added cautiously, "He loves you very much."

"Yeah, I know." He laughed ruefully. "Sometimes I wish I'd had brothers and sisters, someone else to share this responsibility I feel to make him proud and happy. I think I've disap-pointed him."

"Why do you say that?"

He looked uneasy and shifted in his chair before answering. "Dad has this . . . obsession . . . to con-tinue the line, keep Bridal Wreath and the planta-tion in the hands of a Prescott." He took a quick sip of coffee and said, "It doesn't look like that is going to happen."

There was nothing she could say to that so she stared at a picture on the wall beside her. They were both quiet as Zack settled the check and they returned to the pickup parked in front of the building.

"The lunch was wonderful, Zack, and so was the Post House. Thank you," Camille said when he had engaged the gears of the truck and merged with the Saturday afternoon traffic in downtown Natchez.

"You liked it?" he asked, smiling.

"Too much, I'm afraid. Between that lunch and Dearly's Southern cooking, I'm going to be very plump any day now." She was laughing, but she suddenly remembered what he had said the first time she had mentioned her weight. He had commented that she could stand to gain some. She slid her eyes to him, and, to her acute embarrassment, he obviously remembered, too.

"I'd say that the few pounds you've gained have all gone to the right places." His grin was comically lecherous, and she blushed under her apricot complexion. He laughed good-naturedly and reached over to give her knee a playful slap, but Camille caught her breath as his fingers lingered there for an instant longer.

They drove through other areas of Natchez and passed one mansion after another. Camille

remarked on how lyrical the names of the home-
sites were—Auburn, D'Evereux, Fair Oaks,
Dunleith, Hawthorne, Mount Repose, and on and
on. Each home was distinctive in design and character. Some looked like little more than lovely
farmhouses, while others were rich with the flavor
of Southern colonial architecture and complete
with the columns depicting Greek revival design,
as Bridal Wreath did.

"I love the grounds surrounding these homes as
much as the houses themselves. The oaks, magnolias, willows—oh, they're lovely. It must be gorgeous in the spring when the azaleas, dogwood,
forsythia, and wisteria are blooming. Not to mention the bridal wreath!" she added emphatically.

"Yes, it is," Zack confirmed. "It's a shame that
the blooms don't last any longer than they do. But,
if they did, I guess they wouldn't be special. Have
you ever seen Longwood?"

"That's the mansion shaped like an octagon,
isn't it?"

"Yes. It was never finished. Only the ground
floor. It's stood empty all these years. I think they
started construction on it in 1858 and by 1861 it
still wasn't completed."

"It's sad to think that someone put all of his
time and effort into a house and then it was wasted. No one ever shared it. I'd much rather have a
smaller house with a lot of people in it than a large
one that's deserted."

"I think I've just figured you out, Miss Jameson. You like a place with a yard full of trees and a house full of people." He looked over at her. "Am I right?" he asked with a twinkle in his eye.

"I've given myself away, haven't I," she replied, smiling. "I suppose it comes from not having any siblings. An only child can be a very lonely person."

"Then we have that in common, don't we, Camille?" His tone was soft, confidential, and stirring, and Camille looked at him tenderly, answering him with an affirmative nod.

She felt warm and contented. The day had been wonderful. She exulted in being alone with him. As they meandered toward Bridal Wreath, Camille snuggled down deeper in the cracked upholstery of the pickup, unmindful of it as she basked in her newly discovered love for Zack and hoping that his attitude toward her today meant that he was changing his feelings about her. He had been gracious, kind, charming, and almost affectionate. Maybe there was hope for them yet. For two years no other man had been able to exorcise the memory of Zack from her mind. Was it remotely possible that Zack could recall their night together with anything other than bitterness? Would he also remember the bliss they had shared?

They turned into the driveway and bounced over the bumpy surface toward the house. "If I may be so critical, Mr. Prescott, I think it would behoove you to have this road black-topped."

"Oh, you think so, Miss Jameson?" he asked in a haughty manner. Then he grinned and winked at her. "You are exactly right!"

The brakes on the pickup squealed loudly as he applied them. He cut the ignition, silencing the chugging motor and the radio. The sudden stillness added to the indolent atmosphere. The western sun cast long shadows on the lawn and gilded the red and orange autumn leaves of the trees, giving them the appearance of living flames. The air outside was chilly, but the interior of the pickup was warm.

Neither Camille nor Zack moved. They sat silent and close in the narrow confines of the cab. It was intimacy without speaking, without touching. Each savored this quiet privacy, the breathless proximity of the other's body.

As if operating on a synchronized time mechanism, their heads turned to face one another. Slowly, Zack reached across the cab and touched her haloed hair lightly, then moved his hand to cup her cheek. She watched his eyes as they studied her intently. Like two cerulean magnets they held her captive as they started at the top of her head, moved across her own wide, swimming eyes, down her nose and lingered on her parted lips. They shifted to her throat, the base of her neck where she felt her pulse throbbing, and then rested on her breasts. Her nipples were taut and tingling, straining against the soft cotton of her shirt.

Zack's eyes came back to her mouth. His thumb caressed her trembling lips, pressing her bottom lip down gently and raking her lower teeth. "I haven't forgotten it, Camille. I remember vividly how it was with us." His voice was a caress, soft and persuasive and disturbingly honest. He placed his other hand over her left breast and applied gentle pressure. "I feel your heartbeat. You remember it, too."

He crushed her against him, trapping his hand between their bodies. She expected his lips to be as fierce in their possession as his embrace, but they were soft, sensuously teasing her mouth with sipping kisses. He probed her lips with his tongue, but when they were parted, he didn't penetrate them. He settled his lips at the corner of her mouth, and she whispered his name urgently, almost frantically.

His restraint failed him, and he covered her mouth with his own. His tongue met hers with a velvet roughness. The fingers imprisoned between their chests managed to stir her to new heights of sensations. Unconsciously, Camille arched against him, presenting him with easier access to her body. His hands followed its contours while his mouth continued its pleasurable demands. He buried his face in the hollow of her neck, breathing harshly, and rasped, "Camille. Camille, you've bewitched me. Ever since Snow Bird—"

The blast of a car horn caused them both to jump and scramble apart. Zack uttered an expletive under his breath that Camille had never even heard verbalized. When he saw a sleek, silver Porsche pull up beside the pickup, he mumbled another curse and opened his door and stepped down. Left to her own devices, Camille made a hurried, shaken effort to straighten her clothes and smooth her hair before she alighted from the cab.

"Darling, I'm so glad I found you at home," said the tall blond woman posed against the sports car. Camille recognized her immediately as the one whom Zack had escorted to the football game the evening before. She was dressed in a rose-colored knit dress, kid pumps, and a paisley scarf that was tied around her neck with just the right touch of careful negligence.

"Hello, Erica. What brings you out here looking for me?" Zack's voice was friendly enough, but Camille thought she detected a hint of irritation.

"Come and give me a proper greeting and then I'll tell you," the woman purred as Zack put both hands on her shoulders and pulled her toward him, giving her a sound kiss on her voluptuous mouth. Camille's heart fell to the ground, and she wished she could flee to the solitude of the dowager house without being seen. That wish was dashed when Zack turned away from Erica and indicated Camille with his hand. "Erica, this is Camille

Jameson. She is redecorating Bridal Wreath for us. Camille, Erica Hazelett."

"Hello, Mrs. Hazelett," Camille said with little enthusiasm. Under Erica's scrutiny, she was abashedly aware of her casual and comfortable attire. Her hair lay in tumbled curls after Zack's ardent embrace. Were her lips as bruised and swollen after his kisses as they felt? She felt very gauche compared to this immaculate woman.

Erica greeted her in kind and then remarked, "I don't know why Zack found it necessary to hire a decorator to redo Bridal Wreath when he knows that for years I have wanted to get my hands on it and have even gone as far as to offer my services for that task."

"I'm sure you would have done a good job, Mrs. Hazelett, but it wasn't Zack who hired me. It was his father."

"And we know, dear, that Dad doesn't think too much of your taste," Zack quipped, and Erica's lovely mouth tightened into a grim line of exasperation.

"Well, if Miss Jameson is decorating it according to your father's taste, then I can't wait to see it when she's finished," she said caustically.

Camille opened her mouth in surprise at the sarcastic remark and then her eyes took on the golden glow of a cat who recognizes an adversary and the hair on the back of her neck crawled with aversion for Zack's lady friend.

Camille had to admit that Erica Hazelett was a flamboyantly beautiful creature. All the details of her appearance that had escaped Camille last night she took account of now. Her hair was blond, too blond not to have been helped by a weekly rinse. Her eyes were a cool blue, but reflected no depth, no human warmth. She had a long, aristocratic nose between two finely arched brows, and her mouth was wide and sensual. She was tall and thin, with a model's boyish figure, and all of her movements were practiced and languid. She never wasted a movement, Camille realized, as she watched Erica fit herself closely to Zack's body and brush away nonexistent lint from the lapels of his jean jacket. These displays of familiarity stung Camille, and it was only her resolve not to let the woman intimidate her that gave her the courage to stand by and watch Erica fondle Zack.

She was speaking in low, cajoling tones. "Zack, darling, please come with me. I tried to call you earlier, but your servant told me that you were out with Miss . . . what was it again? Oh, never mind. I'll forgive you for not being here when I called if you'll come to the party tonight."

Camille was fuming at Erica's condescending attitude toward her. And calling Simon or Dearly, whichever one she was referring to, a servant! The woman was a snob of the worst sort. Besides being beautiful and obviously sexy, what did Zack see in her? She was so shallow, she was virtually transparent.

"Where is the dinner party being held?" Zack asked in a listless voice.

"Oh, I knew you'd come, Zack!" cried Erica before she raised up on her toes and kissed his cheek. "It's at Melrose, darling, and it's black tie, of course."

"Of course," Zack said dryly.

"You'll need to pick me up about seven. I'm sorry I couldn't give you more notice, but the hostess called me in a panic this morning. One of her eligible males canceled out, and she was left with an empty table setting. I told her I was sure I could coax you into escorting me, but at the same time told her to reassure any unattached females there that you were definitely not 'eligible.' "

"I'll be the judge of that, Erica," Zack warned, but Erica seemed not at all disturbed by his lack of humor.

"Oh, you tease," she admonished as she tapped his chest with a long, manicured finger. "I'll see you at seven, darling." After giving Zack another quick kiss on his cheek and ignoring Camille, she climbed into her sports car and sped out the drive.

"Nice car," Camille cooed cattily before she went up the steps to the front porch. She could hear Zack's mumbled curses as he followed her across the warped boards to the door.

*　　*　　*

It was very late that night when Zack came home. Camille wouldn't have admitted to anyone that she had been unable to sleep until she heard the low throb of his Lincoln's motor as he drove it into the garage.

What had he and Erica been doing until this ungodly hour of the morning? All the joy she had felt over their closeness and the shared intimacy earlier in the day had faded at the sight of the sophisticated Erica and the way she fawned over Zack with apparent results. Hadn't he agreed to go to a dinner party on short notice only because Erica asked him to? And only moments after kissing her with breathtaking abandon! Was he always so acquiescent to Erica's desires? What had he been about to say when Erica's arrival had interrupted him? Was he in love with that superficial, silly woman? If he wasn't, what had kept him in her company until three-thirty in the morning?

She chased these questions through her mind until sheer exhaustion forced her into a restless sleep.

Six

Camille accepted Rayburn's invitation to accompany him to church. She sat beside him in his accustomed pew and tried not to nod sleepily through the sermon. Zack, of course, had not come with them, and she resented the fact that she had been unable to sleep until she heard him come home. He was sleeping late this morning without a care in the world, while she was suffering because of his late date with Erica Hazelett.

When they returned home, Zack was in the parlor amidst the sheet-shrouded furniture and sanded woodwork, surrounded by naked walls stripped of paper. He sat in the only uncovered chair, one foot resting on his other knee, drinking a cup of coffee while reading the Sunday sports page.

"Good morning," he called to them as they came in from the hall. "If you can find a chair, have a seat." He laughed affably, and Camille seethed over his civility. Why couldn't he feel cranky and out of sorts as she did?

"Good morning, son. Are there any good football games being shown on television this afternoon?" Rayburn asked as he deposited his hat and coat on a halltree.

"Yeah, a couple of them. I need to drive out to the plantation right after lunch, but I'll be back in time to watch at least the second half with you."

"Fine," beamed Rayburn, and Camille suddenly felt neglected and out of place in this male-dominated household. What was she doing here anyway? How had all of this come to pass? When had she lost control of her life?

Then her eyes met Zack's for the first time that day. She was shocking to see that his gaze on her was intent, the blue eyes looking at her with an undisguised warmth.

"How are you this morning, Camille?" The confidential tone of voice he used made it seem as if they were alone in the room, in the world. It was soft and gentle and caressing. He had his nerve to act so tender toward her when he had stayed in Erica's company until three-thirty this morning!

"I feel great," she asserted with emphasis.

She saw him take note of the shadows under her eyes and the hollows under her high cheekbones, and Camille knew that her haggard appearance belied her confident words.

Zack was trying to hide a smile as he said simply, "Good."

She turned her back on his smirking face and went to the piano in the other half of the large room. Taking off the dust cover, she sat down on the bench and played memorized tunes until Dearly announced that lunch was ready.

Camille had learned from previous weeks that Sunday luncheon was an event and that it was the only big meal on that day. On Sunday evenings, everyone was more or less on their own to eat leftovers or make themselves a snack. Today was no different. The table was loaded with food. There was a platter of golden fried chicken, a bowl of creamy potatoes, various salads, two vegetable casseroles, a gravy boat full of the rich sauce, and a chocolate cake for dessert.

The food was delicious, but Camille's mind didn't concentrate on the meal as much as it did on the man sitting across the table from her. She had seen the tight fit of the camel slacks Zack was wearing when they walked into the dining room. The navy sweater looked so soft that she was sure it was cashmere. While striving to give her full attention to the moist chocolate cake, her mind strayed to the day in the attic when she had, in the still darkness, stroked the hard muscles of Zack's chest with her fingertips. If she reached up under the sweater now, his skin would be warm, the hair on his chest crisp under her fingers and—

Her fantasy was interrupted when she realized that Zack was watching her and had a knowing smile playing around his mouth. Could he always invade her fantasies? She flushed and lowered her eyes quickly to her plate. Why did he affect her this way?

When she had the courage to raise her eyes again, she caught him giving her the same kind of appraisal she had given him. For attending church, she had put on a tailored brown wool suit with a peach-colored silk blouse underneath. Before they had gone into the dining room for lunch, she had taken off the jacket to her suit and hung it on the halltree along with Rayburn's hat and coat. Under Zack's blue stare, she now remembered that the blouse was somewhat sheer and that if she were going to wear it by itself, she always put on a special bra that covered more completely. This morning, knowing that she was wearing a jacket over it, she had worn another type of bra, one that was sheer and left nothing to the imagination. She had forgotten that fact when she had taken off the jacket.

Zack's eyes lowered to her chest and lingered there for agonizing moments while Camille flushed hotly. If he had reached out and actually touched her, she couldn't have felt his interest more keenly. His stare was like a physical caress, arousing and compelling. Finally, he raised his head and met her amber eyes, lit by an inner fire that she was cognizant of, but unable to control.

She fought letting him see her love so nakedly revealed to him, but her senses were helpless when he looked at her so daringly.

Rayburn broke the spell by pushing back from the table and rescued her from Zack's dangerous hypnotism.

"I'm going to change, then I'm off to the plantation for a while," Zack said jauntily as he left the room, whistling again. Was she so easily dismissed from his mind?

Later, as she lay on her bed and stared at the same page of her book for minutes at a time, she convinced herself that she could erase his vision just as he could hers. Why then did she see him constantly? Why did all of her thoughts always come back to Zack? Zack's soft brown hair, lit by the sun. Zack's blue eyes that could melt her defenses with one warm glance. Zack's hands with the long, strong, sun-tanned fingers that could stroke her flesh with utmost tenderness. Zack's lips . . .

She must have dozed, for when the telephone on her bedside table rang, she started and it took her a few seconds to orient herself.

She answered the telephone on the third ring with a quick "Hello."

"Come over to the main house right away, Camille."

It was Dearly's voice, and it was breathless and

overwrought. The housekeeper hung up immediately after saying those brief words.

Camille had slipped into a pair of brown slacks earlier, but she had trouble stepping into her shoes and pulling on a blazer as she stumbled to the door. Something was dreadfully wrong. Dearly would never have been that peremptory, that abrupt. A premonition of disaster settled in the pit of Camille's stomach as she crossed the terrace with long running steps.

She entered the screened porch and went toward the door leading into the kitchen. She opened it and went in, closing it behind her to keep out the cold air. She turned and gasped at what she saw.

Rayburn was lying on the kitchen floor. His eyes were closed; the fine, chiseled lips hung open, slack; his nose looked pinched; the white hair, usually immaculately combed, stood out at angles around his head; his skin was a sickening yellow-gray color. Simon had straddled Rayburn's stomach and was leaning into his chest. With the heels of his hands, he applied sharp thrusts at regular intervals a few seconds apart to the still chest under him. Rayburn's shirt was opened; his belt and top button of his pants undone. Dearly was standing by the telephone, wringing her hands and crying.

Camille took in the situation at one glance and

asked hurriedly, "Have you already called an ambulance?"

"Yes," Simon answered without breaking the rhythm of his CPR tactics. "Go find Zack. He's at the plantation. Go straight to the hospital. The ambulance will be here in a few minutes. We'll go there—one way or the other."

"The telephone . . . ?"

"No answer out there." He was perspiring profusely, but his voice was calm. He gave a small cry of triumph as Rayburn gasped for breath, and Simon felt a faint pulse under his hand. "Thank God," he prayed.

Camille echoed the prayer, but she wasted no time running to her car, which was parked in the large garage next to Zack's Lincoln.

She got in and turned on the ignition. The car, thankfully, started immediately and she expertly guided it out of the garage and down the driveway. Did she remember the way to the plantation? She must! Over the Mississippi River bridge, through Vidalia, turn north. Yes. She would remember. But how long would it take her, and where on the vast acreage would she find Zack? Oh, God, please don't let us be too late. She gripped the wheel firmly and tried to consciously slow the pounding of her heart. She had to remain calm. She had to be strong for Zack's sake. He would be upset, and she must help him through whatever he would face when they reached the hospital. What if

Rayburn— No! She wouldn't even think about *that* possibility. Simon had started his heart beating again. The ambulance was on its way, had probably arrived just moments after she left. The paramedics would see that he got immediate attention.

She crossed the bridge and sped through the small town, grateful for the lack of traffic on this peaceful Sunday afternoon. Peaceful? How quickly one's well-being can be shattered, how lives can be altered forever in the blink of an eye. Please, God, don't let him die!

She came to the road leading into the plantation sooner than she expected to and turned, almost without braking to slow down. Where to go? She played a hunch and accelerated the car in the direction of the stables. She saw no one to ask about Zack's whereabouts and remembered the ball games being played on television. No one was going to be out and about when they could be indoors watching football. Unjustifiably, she was angered that people would put so much stock in a sport. *Especially at a time like this,* she thought bitterly. She realized her thinking wasn't rational, but these random, nonsensical thoughts kept her from thinking about Rayburn's long body sprawled out on the kitchen floor, vulnerable and lifeless.

She spotted the derelict pickup parked outside one of the barns and whipped her small car up beside it. She didn't cut the motor, but engaged the emergency brake and flung herself out the door, calling Zack's name. She ran headlong into the barn and collided with a man in the dim interior.

"What the—"

"Where is Zack?" She gripped the man's upper arms and arrested his attempt to question her. "It's an emergency. Where is he?"

Apparently he read the alarm in her eyes. He answered her briefly. "He's out riding one of the mares."

"Where?"

"Out that way." He pointed past her toward a large meadow that seemed to stretch to infinity.

"Can you signal him? Do you have any kind of fire alarm, anything?"

"Well . . ." He scratched his head and Camille almost screamed with impatience. "I've got a pistol," he started dubiously.

"Get it and fire it as many times as it will," she commanded.

He did as he was told. Obviously the pistol was already loaded. He brought it outside and fired into the air six times. On the still atmosphere of this Sunday afternoon, the shots resounded and echoed interminably.

He was a mere dot on the horizon when Camille first spotted him, but within seconds, Zack and his mount took shape as he came thundering over the pasture.

He saw Camille while he was still far away, and she could read the puzzled expression on his face.

Then as he got nearer, she saw anguished knowledge dawn on his face as he realized the only emergency that would bring her out to find him and force her to go so far as to alert him with the pistol. He dismounted before the mare came to a complete stop and hit the ground running.

"Dad?" he asked, already knowing her answer.

"Yes, Zack. We're to go to the hospital immediately."

"Get in." He indicated the passenger side of her car. "Ernie, rub down the horse please. Get someone to drive the pickup home for me."

He climbed behind the steering wheel, scooted the seat back several inches to accommodate his long legs, and jerked the car into gear. If Camille had thought she drove fast to get to the plantation, she felt as if her car were flying under Zack's piloting. The landscape was a blur. He cut her time by half on their return trip to Natchez. She was once again thankful for the small amount of traffic.

"What happened?" he asked as he pulled up to a stoplight, cursing when he saw that he must yield to a car full of teen-agers followed by a station wagon with a large family in it.

"I really don't know, Zack. He had a heart attack. Dearly called me at the dowager house. When I reached the kitchen, he was lying on the floor. Simon was straddling him and pushing on his chest. They had already called the ambulance, though it hadn't arrived when I left. I came to get you immediately."

"Was he . . . Did you see if . . ." His voice cracked and Camille impulsively reached over and rested her hand on his thigh. She had dreaded this question, but she knew that she must answer him honestly.

"When I first came in, he wasn't breathing. Just before I left, Simon started his pulse and he took a gasping breath."

"Oh, God," Zack groaned and banged his fist against the steering wheel of the car.

They entered the emergency driveway of the hospital and Zack parked in a vacant place near the door. He and Camille practically ran through the glass door that opened automatically as they stepped onto the rubber mat in front of it. Dearly and Simon jumped up from a green vinyl couch when they saw them. Zack was striding purposefully toward the treatment rooms when Simon grasped his arm and stopped him.

His voice was low, calm, but urgent. "Zack, they won't let you in there, and you can't help anyone by getting in their way. They know what they're doing. Please wait out here with us. Dr. Daniels is already with him. He was here when we arrived."

Camille looked at the rigid lines around Zack's mouth and saw them soften just a bit. The body that had been pulled as taut as a violin string relaxed, then slumped imperceptibly. If she hadn't had a hand on his arm, she wouldn't even have noticed the change. He gave credence to the wisdom of Simon's words.

"What happened?" Zack asked them with the same economy of words that he had used to ask Camille earlier.

Simon didn't answer. Dearly explained the circumstances that had brought them all here. "I was in the kitchen reading through some recipe books when he came in and told me that he had an upset stomach and asked for a bicarbonate of soda. I thought that he looked . . . bad. His coloring and all. I turned around to fix him the soda and then I heard him collapse on the floor. I screamed for Simon, who was there within seconds."

Simon picked up the story. "I was already downstairs. We had been watching the ball game on the television in his bedroom. He was restless and seemed unable to relax. I didn't think too much about it when he said he was going downstairs for something, but after he left, I got a feeling that he hadn't felt well and didn't want to say anything. I followed him down and then heard Dearly call me."

Zack put his hand on the man's shoulder and clamped it tightly. "Thank you, Simon. Whatever happens, I'm grateful to you for being there when he needed you. How was he when they brought him in?"

Dearly was quietly weeping now and Camille led her to the plastic sofa again but never diverted her attention away from the conversation between the two men. She watched Zack closely.

"He wasn't conscious, Zack, but he had a pulse again. Not as strong as we'd like it, but there just the same. They gave him oxygen and he was breathing fairly well. They took him into that room"—he indicated one of the rooms down the hall—"and no one has come out since."

Zack nodded grimly and walked toward the room, though without the imperious purpose he had shown moments before. Simon went to sit beside Dearly, and Camille crossed to Zack. She didn't touch him; she didn't even look at him. She only let him known by her presence that she was available if he wanted her.

They waited for over an hour in tense silence. Zack paced the floor while Camille leaned against the wall. Dearly and Simon sat talking softly together on the sofa. They watched the tragic parade through a city hospital's emergency ward. A distraught couple brought in a little girl with three burned fingers. Two teen-aged boys had run together while playing basketball, and each sported a bloody nose and swollen eyes. They were all treated and left, and still Zack had heard nothing about his father's condition. Though nurses hurried in and out of the room, they would divulge no information, much to Zack's growing impatience.

When the words they longed to hear finally came, it happened so suddenly that the agonizing minutes of waiting vanished in that instant.

The door to the treatment room swung open, and a gray-haired man with horn-rimmed glasses came out, saw Zack, and extended his hand as he strode toward them. Zack clasped the hand as if it were a lifeline—and indeed it was—and asked the important question with his eyes.

"Your father's resting now, Zack, and is—for the present—out of danger."

Zack raked a trembling hand over his eyes and then through his hair before saying gruffly, "Thanks, Doc."

The doctor nodded in acknowledgment and spoke slowly. "It was a bad one, Zack. I won't sugarcoat it for you. He's still in bad shape. I'll put him in intensive care and he'll stay there until I see fit to let him out. It may be several weeks. He's conscious, told me he had goddamned fried chicken for lunch." When he saw that Zack was about to speak, he held up both hands in front of him. "I know, I know, you hate to nag him. Anyway, he'll be monitored twenty-four hours a day. I don't want him to relieve himself without my knowing it." He suddenly became aware of Camille and glanced quickly to Zack before he apologized. "I'm sorry, young lady, for being so indelicate."

"Dr. George Daniels, Miss Camille Jameson.

She's staying at Bridal Wreath and redecorating it for us."

"Ah, yes. Rayburn mentioned you when I saw him at his last checkup. He was looking very forward to your arrival."

"Is there anything we can do, Dr. Daniels?" Camille asked after shaking the strong, sensitive fingers of the doctor.

"Yes. As soon as he's allowed visitors, you can come and sit by his bedside. The sight of your face and body would give any man a reason for wanting to recover." He laughed and Camille blushed, looking timidly at Zack, who was smiling. Dr. Daniels was no fool. He had relaxed them all, and Camille was grateful to the crusty, brusque man for that. She liked him.

She excused herself, leaving Zack and the doctor to their own conversation, and told the anxious Mitchells the news about their employer.

"Why don't the two of you go home. I'll stay here with Zack. I'm sure he won't be leaving any time soon. We'll call you if there is any change in Mr. Prescott's condition."

Actually, they probably had more business staying with Zack than she did, but there was no way on earth she would leave him now.

She turned from the door after waving them off and saw the bed with Rayburn on it being rolled out of the emergency unit on its short trip to the ICU. He was surrounded by professional people. A nurse supported an IV bottle over his arm. When Camille drew closer, she saw the oxygen tubes inserted in his nostrils. His face still retained that unhealthy, waxen sheen, and Camille's earlier alarm returned.

Zack was leaning over his father and clasping one of the pale hands in his own strong, brown ones. Camille couldn't hear what they were saying. Rayburn's voice was weak, but Zack was smiling. Just as they were about to roll the bed away, Rayburn caught sight of her. Much to her dismay and the censure of the nurses, Rayburn motioned her over. Dr. Daniels gave a perfunctory nod of his head when she sought his permission with her eyes. She moved toward the bed and leaned over Rayburn, placing her ear almost directly over his lips so she could hear his hoarse whisper.

She smiled down into his face and nodded her head, then brushed Rayburn's forehead with her lips. The nurses rolled the bed down the hall with Dr. Daniels swaggering behind it.

"What was that all about?" Zack asked her as they followed the entourage at a distance down the hall.

"He asked me to take care of you. He said that you are stubborn sometimes and won't accept help when you need it." She slid her eyes in his direction.

"Oh, yeah? What do *you* think, Miss Jameson?" he asked belligerently.

126

"I think that is probably a fair assessment of your personality. I also think you need a cup of coffee." When he started to protest, she argued, "They won't allow you to see him for a long while yet. Come on," she ordered, taking his arm and steering him in the opposite direction of the ICU ward toward the coffee shop.

"Yes, sergeant," he snapped.

When they were seated at the pink Formica-topped table sipping coffee whose only merit was the fact that it was hot, Zack said seriously, "I haven't had a chance to thank you for what you did today. I—"

"Zack, please. Don't say any more." She shook her head sadly as she gripped the warm cup between her cold hands and stared at the oily, dark liquid it contained. "Do you really think I want your 'thank yous'? After all that's happened between us—"

"Yes," Zack interjected. "Yes, something *did* happen between us." He searched the golden-flecked brown eyes raised to his. They had become luminous with unshed tears. He took her small hand and enveloped it between his. "*Why*, in God's name, Camille, *why* did you leave me that night at Snow Bird?"

He had never overtly mentioned their night together, and, now that it was there, in the open, between them, all the memories came flooding back, suffocating Camille, drowning her in recollections. She longed to reach out and touch the soft curls hanging loosely on his forehead, caress the firm chin and strong jaw line, lay her head against the hard chest, find succor in the strength of his arms. She composed herself enough to speak. "I . . . Utah happened so long ago, Zack. It was another time. I don't want to talk—"

"*I* want to talk about it, goddammit!" The cords of his neck stood out and he spoke between clenched teeth.

"You're upset, Zack. I don't think either of us is emotionally stable enough right now to hash over ancient history." It wasn't what she wanted to say, but she had to be hard in order to save her life. Then she added a cheap shot. She knew it to be that when she said it, but she was fighting for her last shred of dignity. "I don't think it's fair to your father for us to sit here and discuss our problems."

He muttered an expletive, pushed back from the table, and fished in the pocket of his tight jeans for change to leave on the table. As they were walking toward the door of the coffee shop, he gripped her upper arm and turned her around to face him.

His face was bending low over hers when he threatened, "I'll know the reason why, Camille. No woman leaves my bed and makes no explanation. When this is all over, you'll tell me why you did."

He released her abruptly and she staggered before she regained her footing. That's all it was! His male ego had been trampled, and he must

know why she had left him. He didn't care about
her or her feelings. He only wanted his self-image
restored. Apparently, he had had so many inter-
ludes, that a woman sneaking away from him was
unheard of. Camille had remained vivid in his
mind only for that distinguishing reason. She was
the one—the *only* one—who had ever left him!

The words struck her like a physical blow. She
had hoped that maybe Zack had felt a small measure of the tenderness she felt for him. Now she
knew better. She had been a body, nothing more.
An object to satisfy his sexual lust, not a person
with a soul and spirit. When he had awakened to
find that his bed partner for the night had left him,
his ego had been bruised. His pride couldn't toler-
ate that, and he still wanted to know the reasons
behind her desertion.

And yet, even as she raged at him, Camille
knew she loved him. She studied him as he consulted with the nurses and Dr. Daniels as they
came and went out of Rayburn's room all afternoon and evening. Yes, she loved him. What was
she going to do? Over and over, throughout that
interminable day, she asked herself that question.

When she and Zack finally left the hospital, it
was after eleven o'clock. Dr. Daniels assured them
that he would call if there were any change in
Rayburn's condition before morning. They drove
home depleted and silent.

They still hadn't spoken even as they let themselves into the darkened entrance hall. Nor did they speak before Zack took her in his arms and crushed her to him in a punishing embrace.

The lips that came down on hers were brutal, bruising. One hand was tangled in her dark hair, holding her head immobile while he searched her mouth with his tongue as if seeking answers to the questions that plagued him. She berated herself for not fighting him, punishing him as he was punishing her, but her emotions were running too high, too close to the surface. All day they had been pent up, safely stored. The trauma of seeing Rayburn near death on the floor, the hazardous drive to the plantation and back, the tense waiting in the hospital, the argument with Zack, all culminated in her answering his kiss with unrestrained passion. Her emotions sought an outlet, a release, in his arms, his mouth, his heat.

When he accepted her acquiescence, his lips softened, became more persuasive. His mouth pulled gently on her lips, her tongue. He murmured incoherently, or was she making those small pleading sounds? She didn't know, didn't care. His lips trailed to her ear, her neck, and settled against the base of her throat. She threw her head back and allowed him access to her neck and more.

He pulled the silk shirt from the waistband of her slacks and slipped his hands under it. She still wore the same peach-colored blouse without the restrictive bra it required and felt his hands close over the sheer fabric of the one that revealed too much.

"I've got to touch you," he rasped as his hands unclasped the front fastener of the bra, and her breasts spilled into his palms. "Oh, God, Camille," he breathed as he nuzzled her neck. His fingers explored gently, teasing her nipples to a response.

She barely had time to softly cry his name before his mouth descended on hers once again with a renewed passion. His hips fit snugly against hers as he slipped the blazer off her shoulders. He unbuttoned her shirt with maddening slowness, pausing to caress the creamy flesh as it was exposed, bending once to kiss a sensitive spot. The stroking of his tongue generated a shock wave through her body.

Camille reeled against him with mounting desire. She worked feverishly with the buttons of his shirt and finally succeeded in pushing it from his broad shoulders. They both broke away to slip out of their sleeves. When they stood facing each other, naked to the waist, Zack reached up and cupped her face in his palms, running his thumbs lightly over her lips. His eyes were tender, soft, all arrogance and anger vanquished. He adored her with his eyes, sweeping across her features, her flesh, with affectionate delight. "Camille, you're so beautiful. I want you. I need you tonight." His words were little more than an expulsion of breath.

Then one hand lowered and lightly cupped her

Sandra Brown

breast, stroking it softly. The pressure of his hand increased slightly, and, with utmost gentleness, he pulled her forward and pressed her breast against his own warm, naked flesh. She moved into him, the crisp hairs on his chest tickling her, thrilling her. He drew her even closer until her breasts were flattened against the wall of muscle. She could feel the gold cross he always wore around his neck imbedding itself in her skin. The mouth that took hers was promising, tantalizing, yet demanding. Their tongues touched.

"Zack, is everything all right? I heard you come in but didn't see any lights." Dearly's voice seemed to echo for an eternity in the hallway as an arc of light fanned out into the hall when the kitchen door was opened in the back of the house.

Camille retrieved her blouse and jacket from the floor and held them in front of her as she darted into the dining room. She frantically tried to slip on her blouse.

Zack dodged the light by stepping into the deep shadows under the staircase. "Yes, Dearly. We're all right." He cleared his throat and tried again to sound convincing. "We were just talking. Dad's condition is stable. I'll call you if we have any further word."

"Well, I waited up to tell you that there's food in the refrigerator if you want it. Oh, and Mrs. Hazelett called three times." Her tone betrayed a

132

touch of asperity as she divulged this last piece of information.

"Thank you, Dearly. Go on to bed. I'll see you in the morning." They heard the kitchen door swing shut, plunging them into darkness again. Then the back door slammed, signifying that Dearly had gone to her garage apartment where Simon had already retired.

"Damn!" Zack exclaimed under his breath. "I feel like a schoolboy. I'm a grown man and I'm standing here under the stairs necking like a damn fool." He raked his hands through his hair, which only moments before Camille had rumpled with impassioned hands.

"I . . . uh . . . I'll see you in the morning," she stammered as she finished buttoning her blouse.

"Yes, I guess we'd better go to bed," he said. His laugh was harsh and humorless. "*Separate* beds, Miss Jameson," he mockingly assured her with a sweeping bow. "Once again you have been saved from a fate worse than death. Will your luck *never* run out?"

"Ooooh! You are always so superior, aren't you?" His bitter, sarcastic inflection hurt as much as his words themselves. She lashed back, "I suppose you think that I planned all this, that I knew Dearly was in there. Well, I don't care what you think. I'm only glad that she *was* there and that she made her presence known when she did." She stalked to the door then flung back over her shoulder, "Besides, what would Erica think?" She felt smug at having gotten in the last word, but her triumph was short-lived as he called after her.

"I don't know. But I intend to find out. I'm going to call her immediately."

He only laughed as she slammed the door behind her.

Seven

Camille could barely recall afterward that first week that Rayburn spent in the hospital. As hectic and nerve-wracking as they were, the days fell into a grinding routine. She and Zack left Bridal Wreath for the hospital each morning and stayed through late into the evening. Camille would take a break late in the morning, go back to Bridal Wreath, check on the work being done on the house, eat her one balanced meal for the day, and then return to the hospital so Zack could leave for a while.

At first, Dr. Daniels forbade Rayburn having any visitors other than a three-minute visit with Zack about every four hours, but as his patient seemed to improve and gain strength, the doctor granted his permission for Camille to go in, sometimes alone, but often with Zack. These visits seemed to help Rayburn more than any of the strong medication he was taking.

Camille refrained from talking about the restoration of the house when she was in his room, but Rayburn asked questions about it, and she soon found herself giving him detailed progress reports. Each day she received some of the materials previously ordered, and now she had seamstresses making draperies, carpenters making cornices, and paperhangers hanging wallpaper. He wanted to know about it all. She realized just how much this project meant to him.

After a week in the ICU, Dr. Daniels informed Zack that he was moving Rayburn to a private room.

"He's a tough old geezer, Zack. He has a tenacious hold on his life, and that's as crucial to his recovery as medication or surgery or anything else I could do. With proper care and attention to his diet, I think he'll be okay for a while. But I still don't want a parade of people through his room. Rest is still the best medicine right now. Keep an eye on things and, if it gets too crowded in there, I'll slap a 'No Visitors' sign on his door."

Dr. Daniels also mentioned that the stairs at Bridal Wreath weren't good for a heart patient to climb each time he wanted to go to his room. He suggested that other arrangements might want to be made. Camille was consulted.

"What can we do about that, Camille? This is your area of expertise, and I'll guarantee any amount of money required to have something fixed up for him." Zack's eyes had lost some of the haunted anxiety they had reflected for the first few days after Rayburn's attack. His love and concern for his father had been apparent. He stood by hopefully as Camille groped for inspiration.

When the idea came to her, a light shone in the golden depths of her eyes, and her face fairly sparkled as she envisioned what she had in mind. "Yeeeees." She drew out the word. Then excitedly, "Yes, Zack, I think I have an idea that he might like, and it won't cost too much."

"Your first priority was right. He must like it. I'm not sure he'll go for the idea of being ousted from his own room. Maybe we should keep it a secret for a while."

"Okay, but let's call it a surprise rather than a secret. It sounds less devious."

"Agreed." He smiled.

"If it turns out the way I think it will, he'll love it. I'll give it every ounce of talent I have. It'll probably end up being the showplace of the mansion." She laughed. Her enthusiasm was contagious, and Zack joined her laughter. It warmed her heart to see him relax somewhat after being so tense. The lines around his eyes testified that he was tired and hadn't been sleeping well even when he was home for that purpose.

Their encounter in the hallway the night after Rayburn's attack had made them wary of each other. They were like two fencers, choreographed in a strange ballet, thrusting and parrying with each other's words and emotions. Around other people they appeared to be close friends, sharing a common concern over a loved one. In private, they were edgy, uncommunicative, careful.

Camille wasn't nearly as afraid of Zack as she was of herself. She had stormed into her room that night, disgusted with herself for allowing him to make love to her that way. *Love?* No! Love played no part in his embraces. Hadn't he as much as said he only *wanted* her. Then. For the moment. "I need you tonight," he had cried in a soft whisper. He needed a woman, a body. Camille Jameson just happened to be the only one there.

If he had said, "I love you," what would she have done? She admitted ruefully that she would have thrown herself into his arms and begged him never to release her. Her love for him was a part of her, and, though Zack would never return it, she knew that as long as she lived she would love him. She had ever since Snow Bird.

It wasn't fair of him to continue seducing her body when it was her soul that cried out for him. Then she remembered how his lips felt against her own, against her flesh, how his hands were demanding and gentle at the same time, and how his body displayed such evident desire for hers. She confessed that her physical longing was a very real part of her love. But without love, desire became a sham, a surrogate for the real thing, and

Camille couldn't settle for less than love, even with Zack.

She resolved to prevent herself from getting into a situation where his advances would make her susceptible to surrender. She would do her job and be his friend in this time of need, and that was all. Her love for him would be her secret, something treasured in private. She wouldn't allow it to be visible to him or anyone else.

Despite everyone's assurance that Rayburn would be watched closely twenty-four hours a day, Zack insisted that he stay in the hospital room with his father at night.

"He's been hooked up to those machines that monitor everything, but now he's on his own in there. I want to be around if . . . if anything happens." He argued with an army of nurses and then with Dr. Daniels, but he remained adamant.

Camille was worried about him. She could tell by his gaunt face and quivering voice that he was exhausted, and his nerves were frayed like an old rope, ready to snap at any instant as he prevailed upon George Daniels.

"Very well, Zack. You're a grown man, and bigger than I am, so I couldn't physically throw you out," Dr. Daniels conceded grudgingly.

"I'll rest during the day when there are a lot of nurses and doctors around to take care of Dad."

So it was settled, and there seemed to be nothing anyone could do about it.

In the daytime Camille was too involved with the restoration to see Rayburn as much as she would like. She tried to soothe his petulant whining about this when she managed to run to the hospital for a brief visit. It was difficult not to give away the surprise about his new bedroom that was taking up so much of her time. She wanted it to be finished by the time he came home from the hospital. It would be her get-well present for him.

She remembered him telling her how he moved all of his plants into the house during the winter and how crowded it became. She expounded on that idea and decided that, structurally, the screened back porch was the solution to settling Rayburn in a room downstairs. She contacted a carpenter who had the time available to enclose the room. Glass was put inside the screens so that the open-air look was not sacrificed. Camille ordered woven-wood window coverings that could be raised or lowered depending on the natural light desired or privacy required. She wanted to leave him an unobstructed view of the grounds he loved.

She divided the long room in half. One side became a bedroom complete with a small bath that was conveniently connected to the existing plumbing. The other half of the room she made into a den. The floor was covered with indoor-outdoor carpet. His favorite easy chair was recovered in a new, bold fabric using the earth-tones color scheme Camille had chosen. His television set, bookcases, and personal items were moved from the room upstairs. With Zack's hearty approval, a few new pieces were added. Camille and Simon filled the den with plants. She installed a humidifier both for Rayburn's comfort and the health of the tropical plants. Everyone in the household was involved in the project and did their best to hurry along its completion. Camille was satisfied with the results and only regretted that the lovely furniture upstairs, the tester bed, the rosewood armoire, would not be used by the head of the house any longer. But Rayburn's health was far more important than furniture.

Zack liked the new arrangement. During the day, his father would be within calling distance of Dearly as she worked in the kitchen. The downstairs rooms would make it easier on the Mitchells, who were past middle-age, as they helped Rayburn to convalesce. All in all, Camille's idea had been the solution to their problem, and she glowed under Zack's praise when he saw the rooms taking shape.

He had been at the hospital five nights straight, and, when he came home long enough to hurriedly gulp down dinner, Camille was astonished at how fatigued he looked.

Later in her room, she was restless, pacing the floor of the dowager house. Her concern for Zack was no less than her worry over Rayburn. He was too stubborn to admit that he would do his father little good if he became ill, too. She had made the mistake of pointing that fact out to him. After he left Dearly and Simon had sympathized with her for his verbal abuse. It had been a nasty scene before he grabbed his jacket and stormed from the house.

"It doesn't matter," she reasoned with them. "He's so tired, he doesn't know what he's saying."

She couldn't rest, and, after convincing herself that she was doing the right thing, she went into the kitchen of the main house, made a telephone call, raided the refrigerator, and left for the hospital.

Camille opened the door of Rayburn's room apprehensively, but determined. It was dark inside, with only one nightlight giving faint illumination. She could tell by his even breathing that Rayburn was in a deep, drug-induced sleep. Zack was standing by the window. His hands were supporting him against the sill as he leaned his forehead on the cold glass panes.

He turned when she came in, and she saw the surprise on his weary face. "I thought you were a nurse. What are you doing here? Is anything wrong at home?" His voice was tired.

"No. Everyone else is fine. You're the one who looks and feels like hell." He glowered at her from under lowered brows, and she stifled an impulse to laugh.

"Thanks," he said succinctly.

"You're welcome," she replied sweetly. "I brought you a snack. Cold roast beef sandwich, apple, and homemade cookies. Eat it," she commanded. He hesitated only a moment, then sank gratefully into a deep chair. She pulled up a small table and spread the food out for him. "I'll be back in a minute with some milk. No more coffee for you tonight." Without waiting for his protest, she walked smartly toward the door and went through it with a toss of her head.

When she came back after buying a container of milk out of a vending machine, she noticed that the sandwich had already disappeared and Zack was working on the apple. As he chewed, he tried to keep the apple from crunching loudly in the stillness of the room. She suppressed a giggle at his effort and received another dark, glowering look for her attempted levity. He finished the light meal in silence, and drank the milk in one long swallow.

"Very good. Thank you." Zack wiped his mouth with the paper napkin she had brought and began putting the wastepaper in the small brown sack that had held his snack.

"I'm glad you enjoyed it. I'll be right back." She left again, but returned only seconds later. Zack had resumed his position beside the window and was rubbing the back of his neck with one hand and trying unsuccessfully to cover a yawn with the other. Camille walked in with a militant-looking nurse behind her carrying aloft a long, intimidating hypodermic needle.

Camille knew that Zack would think the medication was for his father. When she and the nurse converged on him, trapping him against the window, she noted his bemused look.

"Drop your pants, Zack." Whether he was surprised by her imperious tone or her brazen words, she didn't know, but his baffled look was almost comical. It took tremendous effort not to laugh at him. She kept the muscles of her face drawn into a stern expression.

"What in the hell are you talking about?" he growled.

"I said, 'Drop your pants.' We're going to give you a nice shot to make you sleep." Her voice dripped with that syrupy, insincere gaiety that nurses use on difficult patients.

"Like hell you are," Zack said defiantly.

"Dr. Daniels's instructions. If you insist on staying in this room, you'll stay here asleep. Now, are you going to behave like a good little soldier, or are we going to have to call in an orderly to help hold you down?"

She was sure that at that point Zack would happily have murdered her. No one manipulates a man like Zack Prescott and gets away with it for long.

Zack looked from her to the nurse beside her, who was scowling belligerently, her arms, encased in a starched white uniform, crossed over a bosom of enormous proportions. Her unblinking eyes sat in a face that looked like it had been molded out of clay and baked to diamond hardness. Despite his anger, Camille saw Zack swallow hard at the sight of the needle, and she suppressed another laugh.

"I'm not having any goddamn shot. Not if you call Hippocrates himself in here to give it to me." The muscles of his jaw were working, and he was clenching and unclenching his fists at his sides. Camille recognized the signs. He was about to blow.

"In that case, I'll give you one alternative." She turned to the nurse. "Please bring in the bed." The nurse snorted in disdain at Zack and then left the room on silent feet. She moved with surprising agility for a woman of her size.

"I've asked them to bring a rollaway bed in here for you. I'll stay awake and keep an eye on Mr. Prescott. You have my word on that, but, Zack, you must get some rest. Please. For your sake as well as that of your father's. If you collapse from exhaustion, what good are you to him? And he can't get well if he's worried about you. I promised him I'd take care of you, and I intend to keep that promise."

He sighed and ran his hand wearily through his tangled hair. "You'll stay awake? All night?"

"Until you awaken in the morning," she promised.

Just then the door opened, and an orderly

wheeled a small bed into the room. He left as silently as he came.

Zack looked at Camille and then at the figure on the hospital bed, who miraculously had slept through all of the commotion. Camille saw Zack's shoulders slump and read the resignation on his face. Then he smiled crookedly. "That chair isn't half bad if you get tired enough." He indicated the soft, imitation leather chair. He crossed to the bathroom and went in, shutting the door behind him. Camille settled herself in the chair, preparing for her nocturnal vigil. Zack turned off the light in the bathroom as he came out and went to the bed, looking down on it skeptically.

"I don't think I'm going to fit on this damn thing," he complained as he pulled off his shoes.

Camille laughed softly. "You'll be asleep so fast you won't even notice." She leaned back in the soft chair then sat bolt upright when she saw Zack shrug out of his shirt and unbuckle his belt. "What are you doing?" she asked in a voice that had risen an octave.

"What does it look like I'm doing? I'm taking my clothes off. Should I have been a gentleman and asked you to turn around?"

"But . . . but you can't sleep in here like . . . that," she sputtered.

"This was your idea, remember, Miss Jameson. You told me to drop my pants. I'm sure I won't offend Nurse Stone Face. I think she's seen it all."

He pulled off his jeans without a second's hesitation, and Camille flushed hotly, averting her eyes.

"Aren't you going to come kiss me good night?" he taunted from across the dim room.

"No! I am not!" she exclaimed. His only response was a light laugh. She heard the springs creak, the rustle of the crisp sheets as Zack adjusted himself to the short bed, one muffled curse, then it was silent. As she had predicted, his even breathing just moments later indicated that he had fallen asleep as soon as he allowed himself to lie down. Well, her mission was accomplished, but she was on edge. Everything had been going her way until he had undressed. Dim though the room was, the darkness didn't completely hide his magnificent physique from her eyes. She remembered seeing him lying on the wide bed in the condominium at Snow Bird with only the firelight covering his body. The thought sent disturbing shivers over her, and she shifted uncomfortably in her chair.

The night hours dragged by, the monotony interrupted only by the nurses' periodic visits to Rayburn's bedside. Camille was unreasonably peaceful sitting in the chair or standing near the window, for every minute that she was here, Zack was healthfully sleeping. When the first rays of daylight began to permeate the room, she closed the blinds on the windows and the room was once again shrouded in darkness. She wanted this night to go on for as long as it could.

About half an hour after dawn, she went into the bathroom, carefully shutting the door behind her before turning on the light and switching it off again before opening the door. She was creeping back across the room toward the chair, passing Zack's small bed, when his hand shot out from under the covers and clutched one of her legs around the knee. She clamped a hand over her mouth to keep from screaming in fright and stumbled against the bed, falling across Zack.

She righted herself and glared down into his shadowed face. "You scared me half to death!" she hissed. "It's a wonder I didn't scream this hospital down. And how would you have explained my terror?" He shrugged, and she could see that he was grinning broadly. "Let me go," she gasped as he tightened his hands around her waist.

"No."

"Yes!"

"No!"

"Zack, please. Someone may come in."

"I know the hospital's schedule by now. We have time for me to pay you back for last night." He pulled her down on top of him, and Camille tried frantically to tug on the bottom of her skirt. It had inched its way up to the middle of her thighs during their scuffle. She attributed the unnatural pounding of her heart to the fact that he had startled her, and not that she was lying on top of him with only a sheet and a brief pair of underwear covering him.

"Don't—" she protested, but the word was smothered when Zack's mouth claimed hers. His arms were like steel bands across her back. She resisted, bracing herself on her hands, stiffening her arms, fighting to keep her body from touching his.

His lips were persuasive, and, with the ardency of his kiss, Camille felt her limbs weakening as the warmth of his seeking tongue spread a liquid fire through her veins, melting her resolve, clouding her mind, obscuring her will. She collapsed against his chest with a moan. His arms relaxed their iron grip on her and started caressing her back with a tenderness that was even more binding than his previous stronghold.

"Did I ever tell you what a cute bottom you have?" he asked against her lips as his hands moved under her skirt and slid over the object of his admiration. The warmth of his hands moving over her silky panty hose was intoxicating.

"No! You didn't tell me any such thing. I would have slapped your face," she objected without conviction. He was kissing her again, and her senses were drowning in an ocean of desire.

"Zack, please don't kiss me like this," she pleaded when he finally moved his mouth from hers in order to explore the region behind her ear.

"I'm sorry," he chuckled. "This is the only way I know how to kiss."

"You know what I mean," she persisted as she raised herself over him. He used her movement to turn her over on her back so that now he was looking down on her. The sheet had fallen to his hips and the hair-matted chest was on a level with her flushed face. The golden cross dangled from its chain before her eyes. She was breathless. He stroked back her tangled curls and said with a soft laugh. "As I recall, the first bed we shared was quite a bit larger than this one."

She disengaged herself from his arms and was off the bed before he could react. "I told you that I didn't want to talk about that," she cried vehemently, then glanced toward Rayburn's bed to see if she had roused him. Thankfully, he was still sleeping heavily. "Every time you mention Utah, it proves just how insensitive you are. I asked you not to discuss Snow Bird anymore." She was unsuccessfully adjusting her clothing with trembling fingers.

"Well, I don't always do what you ask, do I?" he whispered harshly as he came out of the bed and started toward her. "I want to have this out here and now. Was spending the night with me in Snow Bird so odious to you? You make me sound like a hoard of Vikings looking for the village virgins and you being the only one found. I don't remember it that way. You weren't raped, Camille.

150

I don't recall you screaming, or kicking, or biting . . . well, maybe a little biting," he added with a wicked glint in his eye as he rubbed a spot on his shoulder. Camille gleaned his implication and was aghast.

She stamped her foot. "You're despicable. No gentleman." Then she groaned, turning her head away. "And I can't stand here and talk to you any longer if you don't put some pants on." She hated the tremor in her voice and tried to steady it as he mumbled, "Oh, hell." He fumbled in the darkness for his jeans and, finally finding them, dragged them on and zipped them quickly.

"Is that better?" He mocked her modest shyness.

"Yes, thank you," she said primly.

"You're welcome," he answered in kind, and Camille hated him for his coolness.

"I want to know what was so urgent that you left me without so much as a good-bye. I want to know *now*!" There was no mistaking his imperative tone. All teasing was finished.

"I . . . I was . . . ashamed, humiliated. I went to bed with a perfect stranger and you took . . . It is the only thing a woman . . . It should have belonged to the man I'll marry." She was crying now but couldn't help herself. "What if I had gotten pregnant?" She saw his face go completely blank then he groaned, "Oh, God—" She was quick to reassure him. "No, I didn't but I could have. I wasn't . . . protected. I had never . . . you took—"

"I didn't exactly *take* anything, Camille. I didn't know you had never been with a man. If you had told me, I would have left you alone." He raked one hand through his hair and rubbed the other one across his chest. "No, I wouldn't've," he admitted with a sigh. Then impatiently, "Hell, I don't know what I would have done, and it's useless to surmise. It happened the way it did. Nothing can change that. And truthfully, I can't say that I regret sleeping with you."

"That's the difference with men and women, Zack. At least this woman. It was just a casual thing with you. I ruined myself. Every time I think about it, I feel cheap and dirty. No decent man will ever want me. I have no self-respect anymore so how can I expect anyone else to respect me?"

"Ruined? Cheap? Dirty?" His volume rose with each word. "Well, thanks a helluva lot. I didn't think my lovemaking was so bestial that it could reduce someone's self-esteem to such a low level." He was slinging on the rest of his clothes, his hair in wild disarray around his head. He was furious, and Camille knew the effort he was exerting not to shout at the top of his lungs. Dressed, he came toward her and grabbed her shoulders. "When you and that *decent* fellow finally get together and you're tearfully explaining to him your lost virginity at the hands of a base, sex-starved maniac, explain this, too." He crushed her body to his. It was a deep, insulting kiss, totally lacking in the warmth and tenderness of those just minutes before. When he had thoroughly plundered her mouth and moved his hands over her in a demeaning way, he shoved her from him and went toward the door. Just then the nurse who had threatened him with the needle the night before came in with Rayburn's breakfast tray and morning medication.

"God! Don't you ever go off duty?" Zack roared as he went through the door, brushing past her immense bulk and almost upsetting the tray in her arms.

Camille, under the nurse's speculative stare, hurriedly gathered her purse and coat and fled, asking the nurse to tell Rayburn that she would be back later.

Eight

*T*he dreadful scene in the hospital room left Camille feeling even more vulnerable with Zack than before. He had the power to hurt her deeply, strip her of her defenses, and this gave him a frightening hold over her. She kept away from him as much as possible lest he see how he affected her.

They spoke to each other with the cold politeness of strangers, and only when forced to speak at all. They tacitly agreed that from that night on, she would relieve him on alternate nights in Rayburn's room. The rollaway bed was left there for them to use while spending the night with him.

After another week, Zack finally conceded that Rayburn was recovering well enough to stay alone. He was now able to take short strolls up and down the halls, usually accompanied by an attractive nurse, all of whom had developed deep crushes on this white-haired Southern gentleman.

Camille continued to visit Rayburn at least once a day, although she was busy with redecorating the house. It seemed that even the most professional of workers she had hired needed her to answer myriad questions, or give her advice, or offer her approval. As exhausting as her constant vigilance was, she would rather the artisans make sure they were doing something exactly to her specifications than to have them do it wrong and necessitate correction.

These final phases of restoration were providing a glimpse of how lovely the house was going to be when completed. Camille was pleased with all her choices and was anxious for Rayburn to see their planning come to fruition. She inferred that Zack's noncommittal grunts indicated his favor. She was feeling confident about her work on Bridal Wreath and congratulating herself on her excellent taste.

Then the hammer fell.

Early one afternoon she noticed Zack standing in the wide hall looking into the dining room. His hands were on his hips, his booted feet planted wide apart. He had apparently just come in from the plantation for he still had on mud-splattered jeans and a worn jean jacket. He held a battered hat in one of his hands and Camille was reminded of her first day at Bridal Wreath when he had confronted her in this same stance. It was still intimidating.

"Miss Jameson," he said crisply when he saw her approaching. "What in the hell is this?"

Camille shrank from the fierce blue gaze he fixed on her and looked toward the dining room. What was he referring to? She noted that the contract painters were almost finished with one wall of the room.

"They're painting the wall," she answered simply. "We decided not to use wallpaper. It was stripped off weeks—"

"I know what they're doing. I'm well aware of the fact that the wallpaper has been stripped off." His tone was measured, extremely polite and condescending, much like one would use to speak to an incurable, helpless imbecile. "I'm talking about that ungodly color they're smearing on my walls!"

Camille had selected the deep, forest green after picking out that color in the dining room's area rug. The priceless Aubusson rug was an original piece in the house and still retained its beauty. She wanted to keep it in the room but add a touch of modernity to the decor. The seat cushions of the dining room chairs were being covered with a fabric that blended the dark green with shades of beige and peach. It was a contemporary color scheme, but would harmonize beautifully with the colonial architecture of the house.

She faced Zack and said with as much aplomb as she could muster under his withering stare, "It's called hunter—"

"I don't give a damn what it's called. I hate it. I'll feel like I'm eating in a bayou. I've seen swamp water a prettier shade of green than this!" As he gestured wildly with his hand, he accidentally let go of his hat. It sailed across the room and plopped into an open can of the green paint. He blasted the walls with an expletive that would have made a sailor blush. Camille would have loved to laugh as she watched his hat slowly sink into the paint can, but the furious face he turned back to her froze any humor in her throat before it had a chance to escape.

She swallowed and tried to keep her voice from trembling as she explained. "Zack, it won't look so dark when the woodwork is painted white. There won't be any heavy drapes. I'm having a cornice made in the same fabric that will cover the chair seats. Only white shutters will cover the windows. It will be beautiful, I assure you. The green is a very popular, contemporary color."

"For Christmas Day it's great. What do we do with it the other three hundred and sixty-four days of the year?"

His sarcasm stung and she realized that by now the painters had put down their brushes and were listening with avid interest to the argument. Simon and Dearly had come out of the kitchen and were standing in the hall, Dearly twisting her hands anxiously. The lady who had been hired to make drapes for the parlor had ceased her measuring and was witnessing the scene. If Zack's intention was to humiliate her in front of everyone and get it spread all over Natchez that his decorator had appalling taste and didn't know her own field, he was accomplishing just that. She tried one more time to be reasonable.

"There are any number of ways to decorate around it. In the spring you use bouquets of pastel flowers, in the winter, use white, in the fall, gold and copper mums would be—"

"That is all very interesting, but the bottom line is that I don't like it. Change it." With that rude interruption, he turned on the heels of his boots and stalked down the hall.

"I will not!"

The words were out before Camille had time to weigh her angry response. She had tried to be calm, reasonable, and prevent a scene, but he chose to continue with his stubborn dominance. She straightened her spine, and golden sparks flashed out of the eyes that faced Zack defiantly as he turned and looked at her.

His hands clenched at his sides. His jaw worked for several seconds before he said levelly, "May I remind you, Miss Jameson, that I am footing the bills for this restoration. I certainly think that entitles me to an opinion. And, in case you have forgotten, this is my house."

"That is true, Mr. Prescott, but may I remind you that it was your father, not you, who hired me.

It was with his consultation that I chose this color, and, unless he sees fit to change it, it remains the way it is."

"When hell freezes over, Miss Jameson."

"So be it, Mr. Prescott." He took a few striding steps toward her, and she held up her hands as if to halt him. "In deference to your obvious dislike of our choice and your lack of confidence in my abilities and judgment, I'll concede this: If, after the room is completed and your father agrees with your opinion, then I will change it any way you wish—at my expense." A heavy expectant silence hung in the air. Zack didn't speak but only stared at her in a terrifying way. Finally she looked pointedly toward her hired workers, and they immediately scurried back to work. Simon and Dearly wisely retreated.

As she brushed past Zack on her way down the hall, he reached out and grabbed her arm. "You also owe me a new hat," he growled.

"Go to hell," she replied sweetly, her voice dripping with sarcasm. She extricated her arm from his grasp and sauntered down the hall.

It came as a surprise when one day at lunch he asked her to go to the hospital with him that afternoon. Almost two weeks had gone by since the night she had confronted him in Rayburn's room, two weeks since their argument about Snow Bird and his wounding insults. It was only a few days since they had had their altercation over the dining room. They had not spoken to each other after that, but managed to stay out of the other's way.

Her face must have registered her surprise for he said quickly, "It wasn't my idea. Dad asked that you and I come together this afternoon. I've no idea why."

That was all he said as they ate Dearly's delicious chicken salad in the small breakfast room off the kitchen. When he got up from the table, he asked, "How soon can you be ready?"

"Give me half an hour."

"Fine," he replied and left the room.

Tears of frustration and hurt prickled her eyelids, and she brushed them away impatiently before Dearly, who was clearing the table of dishes, could see them. In only a few more weeks the house would be completed, and she would be free to leave Zack forever. She would no longer be subjected to his ridicule and humiliating taunts. Why wasn't she relieved by that thought? Why, for some reason, did it plunge her into deeper despair?

"When are you leaving for the hospital, Camille?"

Dearly's question startled Camille out of her reverie. "What? Oh. In about half an hour, I think," she answered absently.

"Then you'll be getting there about two o'clock?" Dearly persisted.

"Well . . . yes, I guess so. Why?"

"Oh, nothing. I was just wondering. I have some shopping to do this afternoon, and I didn't want to be gone if you should need me for anything."

Camille was too distracted by her own distress to give attention to the housekeeper's curious behavior. She had enough problems to worry about without dwelling on Dearly's idiosyncracies.

She went across the terrace to the dowager house and changed clothes. A pair of designer jeans was fresh from the cleaners, the crease straight and crisp as she pulled them on. She slipped into a turquoise silk shirt that had full sleeves gathered tightly by deep cuffs, and slid a narrow gold belt through the loops of her jeans. She brushed her hair vigorously. The humidity wasn't too bad today so she allowed it to do as it wished, which was to curl around her shoulders softly and frame her face with errant tendrils. She tried to convince herself that going with Zack was of no consequence, but she took special care with her makeup and even sprayed on a woodsy scent that reminded her of the late autumn day. She shrugged into a soft brown leather blazer and was ready.

Zack was already standing by his navy-blue Lincoln when she came down the porch steps, and he stepped to the passenger side and held the door for her. They drove to the hospital in silence. She was painfully conscious of the man beside her though she strived for indifference. He, too, was wearing jeans, the slim European cut flattering his lean hips and long, muscular legs. He had on an open-collared sport shirt and a camel sport coat. Today, he had left his cowboy hat at home, and his hair fell in careless waves around his aristocratically shaped head. His profile was near perfect, Camille thought as she covertly studied him from across the luxurious interior of the car. Inadvertently, she sighed, and he turned, catching her at her scrutiny. She looked away quickly, but not before she read contemptuous humor in the azure depths of his eyes.

"Have you seen Rick O'Malley lately?" Zack's question was casual but took her completely by surprise.

"I have a date with him tonight." Camille had seen little of Rick since the night of the football game. His work at Bridal Wreath was finished, and, if there was an odd job to do on the floors of the mansion, the elder O'Malley came alone. Rick had called earlier in the week and after considerately inquiring about Rayburn's health, asked her to go to the movies with him this Saturday. She had accepted his invitation not only because she liked him, but because the tension at Bridal Wreath had become so unbearable that she needed an evening out.

"I've always liked Rick," Zack said. "He's a good man. Decent." He stressed the adjective and slid a derisive glance in her direction. Then he added blithely, "Of course, you may want to ask him about his love affair with a married woman." Camille jerked her head around to face him. "Don't look so skeptical. It's common knowledge and has been going on for years." He whipped the car into a parking space, braked abruptly, and got out of the car before Camille could respond to his shattering and unbelievable piece of news.

They took the elevator to the fourth floor, and, the moment they stepped off, Camille noticed an atmosphere of anticipation that was almost palpable. She and Zack passed the nurses' station, and several of the women tried to suppress giggles and twittered together like the wallflowers at a high school dance. Camille looked up at Zack quizzically, but he only shrugged and continued his long stride down the corridor.

He stopped in front of Rayburn's door and pushed it open for her. She took one step inside then halted so suddenly that Zack ran into her from behind.

Camille couldn't believe it! The whole room was filled with flowers—not the flowers that Rayburn had received from well-wishing friends, but huge baskets of roses, chrysanthemums, and orchids, sprinkled delicately with baby's breath and delicate fern fronds. Candles glittered from ornate brass holders holding either tall tapers or glowing votive lights. The hospital bed was gone. Standing where it should have been was a white wrought iron arch decorated with flowers and greenery.

Under the arch, Rayburn stood regally in blue silk pajamas and a velour robe. On his arm was a lovely, small woman whose face was wreathed in smiles when Camille walked in.

"Mother!" she exclaimed hoarsely.

Standing on the other side of her mother was a man whom Camille recognized to be the minister of the Prescotts' church, and by his side was a grinning Dr. Daniels, looking devilishly pleased with himself. The room was filled with other doctors and nurses, including Nurse Stone Face, as Camille had come to think of her after Zack dubbed her with that name. Everyone was grinning broadly at Camille and Zack. He was peering over Camille's shoulder, apparently as stunned by the spectacle as she. Camille heard someone sniffling daintily into a handkerchief and turned to see Dearly standing beside a beaming Simon, who had one arm draped comfortingly across his wife's plump shoulders.

"What the—" Camille heard Zack mutter near her ear before Martha Jameson rushed over to her daughter and embraced her warmly.

"Camille, sweetheart, you look positively radiant. I'm so happy for you. When Rayburn telephoned me about you and Zack falling in love at first sight, I was surprised to say the least! I wanted to call you immediately and get all the lovely details, but he asked me to refrain so he could plan this little get-together. And this is Zack!" She moved Camille aside and took both of Zack's hands in hers, looking up at him with admiration. "He's as handsome as I envisioned him to be. You always were so particular about men, Camille, so I knew he would be good-looking. I was beginning to worry that you would never find anyone 'perfect' enough!

"Zack, I'm Martha Jameson. I have every confidence that you'll take good care of my daughter. Of course, I was initially concerned about the difference in your ages and the brief period of time you've known each other, but Rayburn assured me of your steadfast love. If you're anything like your father, I know you're a perfect gentleman. Please call me Martha."

Zack shook hands with Martha and permitted her to kiss him on each cheek. Camille could tell by his blank expression that he was completely baffled.

"Come on now, dears, don't be shy. Everyone is waiting for you." Martha linked her arms through Camille's and Zack's and practically dragged them into the room until they stood in front of Rayburn, whose eyes sparkled under the snowy white eyebrows.

"What the hell is going on?" Camille heard Zack whisper in Rayburn's ear as he hugged him.

Rayburn's answer wasn't confidential. Indeed,

he intoned it loud enough for everyone to hear. "Son, I just couldn't let you and Camille put off your getting married any longer on my account. I know you were both making the sacrifice willingly, but I felt so guilty about it, that I took matters into my own hands and planned this surprise wedding for you."

Camille felt every ounce of blood in her veins rushing to her head; her ears were on fire; and she would have collapsed had not Zack moved closer and lent her support with his own trembling body.

"This isn't what I always dreamed your wedding would be like, darling," Martha said. "But I think this is even better. It's certainly different and something you can tell your children and grandchildren about. And you look just as beautiful in jeans as you would in a long, white dress. I'm sure Zack doesn't mind." Martha was touching Camille's face and stroking her hair with maternal affection and pride as she chirped merrily.

This must be a dream, Camille's mind was screaming. *In a moment I'll wake up and have a good laugh over this funny dream. Or nightmare.* She dared not look at Zack. Was he in this dream, too? Whose dream was it, his or hers? She tried hard to suppress the hysterical laughter she felt bubbling up in her throat.

"I don't know what—" Zack started before Rayburn interrupted him.

"You see, son, I was feigning sleep that morning a couple of weeks ago when you and Camille were in here discussing Utah." He paused momentarily to let Camille and Zack absorb those fateful words, then continued. "You were talking about how nice it would be to honeymoon at Snow Bird where you had both been before." Camille stifled a short gasp. "I could tell by your conversation that you regretted not getting married right after you met. Love happens that way sometimes. It may take only one day—or one night." He paused again. He was letting them know that he had heard everything and that he understood fully what had happened in Snow Bird two years ago. He was also using implicit language. No one but the two involved could catch the true meaning of what he was saying.

"You're a responsible man, Zack, and have always tried to do the right thing. I don't want your responsibility toward me and my illness to keep you from doing the right thing by Camille. I couldn't live with the burden of keeping you two apart when you so obviously should be together."

His expectation was clear to Camille and Zack. Rayburn knew that she had lost her innocence with Zack, and now he was expecting his son to act like the honorable Southern gentleman he had raised him to be and marry the poor, ruined girl. The benign, thoughtful, kind gentleman that people saw when they looked at Rayburn was in the same body with a tough, powerful, forceful man. He had an iron will, and, for the first time, Camille was seeing that will enforced. The usually merry blue eyes under his Santa Claus eyebrows were glinting like steel, daring his son to balk at the plan that he had taken it upon himself to put into action.

He glanced at Camille kindly, then fixed his son with a stare and held it for long moments. When he saw that Zack was evidently not going to object, he rubbed his palms together energetically. "Well, let's get started. We're keeping the Reverend waiting. He has a golf game this afternoon."

Everyone laughed as the principals took their places. Zack and Camille stood facing the minister under the arch after her mother hurriedly pushed a bouquet into her clammy, cold hands. Rayburn and Martha stood on either side of them.

"Oh, Zachary, I almost forgot. Here is your mother's ring. I had Simon bring it. I'm sure she would have loved Camille and would want her to have this ring. Camille, if you prefer another, I'm sure Zack will get you one, but please indulge an old man and use this one in the ceremony."

Camille looked down at the wide gold band lying against his calloused palm and choked back a sob. "I . . . I couldn't hope for another as lovely. Thank you."

He was pleased with her response and blinked back tears of his own before he could speak again. "Camille, you remember meeting Reverend

Collins after church one Sunday," he said in way of introduction.

"Yes. Hello, Reverend Collins," she wheezed.

"Hello, Camille. I didn't know that the very next time I saw you, I'd be marrying you! Hello, Zack."

"Reverend Collins."

"Are you nervous?" the minister asked anxiously.

"No," was Zack's curt reply.

"Ah, good. Here we go then. We'll sign the license after the ceremony."

He proceeded, and, in a matter of minutes, Camille Leanne Jameson and Zachary Benson Prescott became husband and wife. She was married to the man she loved, but at what price? He would resent her for the rest of his life. He had been trapped into marrying a girl whom he looked upon as no more than a one-night fling. What of Erica Hazelett? Wasn't Zack in love with her? She couldn't have prevented the ceremony by crying out what she knew to be true any more than Zack could have strenuously objected in front of this bizarre assembly. He had been coerced, and he would never forgive her for it.

Camille had repeated the vows like a wind-up doll, performing like an automaton in a programmed way. Zack's voice had been clear and level. At least he wasn't giving away his hatred toward her in front of everyone. But what would he do when they were alone?

"You may now kiss your bride, Zack," prompted the minister.

It was over and she was facing Zack for the first time since they had entered the room so innocently. How much had happened in the space of a few minutes! Her whole station in life had changed.

She raised her eyes slowly and met his blue gaze. She hadn't expected the small ray of affection that she saw there, nor the slight smile on his patrician lips. They completely unnerved her, and her lip began to quiver uncontrollably as she felt tears sting her eyes. He was pretending kindness. Why couldn't this be for real? *Why can't he love me the way I love him?*

Zack must have noticed that she was about to burst into tears, because he stopped them with his kiss. It was light at first, with their lips barely touching, but it grew into a tender blending of their mouths as his arms went protectively around her.

When at last they broke apart, everyone applauded and started chattering excitedly as the caterer wheeled in a long table complete with wedding cake and champagne.

Camille was swept away by the throng of wedding guests. She introduced her mother to those few she herself knew, responded to the obligatory toasts, and fed the first bite of wedding cake to Zack, who was going along with all of the foolishness as if nothing at all were wrong between them.

Before he left for his golf game, Reverend

Collins pulled them aside and had them sign the marriage license, which a friend of Rayburn's had secured for them. "I understand that both of you gave blood here at the hospital last week during their donation drive. Dr. Daniels surreptitiously had all of that checked out for you. Congratulations, Zack. I think you have a beautiful bride. Camille dear, best wishes. I hope I'll soon be christening a lot of little Prescotts." If Zack's arm had not been firmly around her waist, she probably would have fainted.

She was distressed to learn that her mother was due back in Atlanta that evening. "I just came for the day, dearest. I wouldn't have missed it for the world, but I really do need to get back. Have you forgotten that we have a business to run? Besides, who wants their mother around on their wedding night?

"Zack, I'm counting on you to bring her home as soon as Rayburn is well. I want to give you a party and introduce my new son-in-law to all our friends. Rayburn has invited me to Bridal Wreath for Christmas. So I'll be seeing you soon."

Dr. Daniels had met her mother at the airport and was planning to take her back to catch a return flight. Before they left, he imperiously ran everyone out of Rayburn's room, announcing that the party was over and that this was still a hospital with a lot of sick people in it. The caterer gathered up the tools of his trade, promising Camille that he would have the flowers delivered to Bridal Wreath so that she could enjoy them there. The hospital bed was wheeled back in, and Nurse Stone Face shooed everyone out as she got Rayburn back into his bed.

Camille clung to her mother one last time and kissed her on the cheek. "Dear, I only hope that you are as happy in your marriage as I was in mine. I think Zack is perfect for you. Make lots of gorgeous babies for Rayburn and me."

"Young Prescott will see to that, you can bet, Mrs. Jameson." Dr. Daniels winked broadly at Camille and dug an elbow in Zack's stomach. "Come along now, we don't want you to miss your airplane."

They walked down the corridor chatting amiably, and Camille stood alone with her husband. Husband! All that the word denoted came washing over her, inundating her with panic. She had the mad desire to run after her mother and cling to her.

As though divining her thoughts, Zack gripped her elbow and led her back toward Rayburn's room. "I want to talk to my father," he growled, but with a forced smile for the benefit of the nurses and doctors who were now going about their business in the halls but still eyeing the newlyweds.

They reached the door of Rayburn's room and met Nurse Stone Face as she was coming out. "Where do you think you're going?" she asked haughtily.

"We're going in for one final word with my father. If you don't mind." Camille knew by the rigid lines around his mouth that Zack was trying hard not to lose his temper. It was becoming a taxing effort.

"Well, I do mind, Mr. Prescott. He's asked me not to let anyone in. He's exhausted after the events of this afternoon. I've just given him a shot to make him sleep and he's probably already dropped off. I won't permit you to go in and get him all excited again."

Zack expulsed his breath in extreme agitation. "Very well, we'll see him first thing in the morning."

He turned, and, taking Camille's arm, steered her toward the elevator. They stood in silence as they watched the light above the door illuminate the numbers of the floors as it made its way up to them. They stared as if the mechanism were the most fascinating thing in the world. When the doors opened, they stepped into the cubicle, and Mr. and Mrs. Zachary Prescott rode down to the first floor without speaking, without touching, without even looking at each other.

Nine

"It's still early yet for dinner. Did you have anything planned for this afternoon?"

Camille was so apprehensive about Zack's unpredictable mood that she actually jumped when he asked her the question as he swung his car out of the hospital parking lot. As far as she could tell, his voice was controlled and revealed no anger.

"I . . . uh . . . I had planned to do some shopping at the mall. There are a few things I needed, but—"

"Then we'll go shopping. Dearly asked me if I would take you out to dinner. She and Simon are busy at home moving your things into the main house."

The corners of his mouth lifted into the semblance of a smile, and he glanced at her to see if the implications of what he'd said registered. They had—all too well. She swallowed convulsively and only nodded in response as she twisted the unfamiliar gold band around her finger.

He parked the car in the vast acreage of the

parking lot, and they walked into the shopping mall whose modernity was somehow incongruous with the antique flavor of Natchez. None of the citizens seemed to mind this variance for the mall was full of shoppers. Zack took a possessive hold on Camille's arm as they wended their way through the crowd. Would anyone have believed that this was what a couple would find to do only hours after being married?

Camille stopped short when she saw another couple coming toward them. She cried, "Rick!" and put both palms up to her face when she remembered that she had a date with him tonight! Now she was a married woman!

He appeared to be just as embarrassed as she. Did the small, black-haired young woman standing with him have anything to do with his abashment? The girl had a sweet face and big brown eyes that seemed almost liquid and held the same sadness that sometimes characterized Rick's own.

"Hello, Rick, Laura." Camille was glad that Zack was taking command of the situation. "Laura Wimberly, I'd like for you to meet Camille. She and I were married this afternoon. You two can be among the first to congratulate us."

There was a momentary stunned pause. Rick looked first at Zack as if he had grown two heads, then at Camille, who expressed an apology with her eyes.

"Well, that's great, you two!" Rick said heartily.

Camille thought that his sentiment was sincere. "Zack, congratulations. Camille, best wishes. You couldn't have found a better man than Zack Prescott. I mean that."

"Thank you, Rick."

"Mrs. Prescott, Rick has told me so much about you. I'm glad I've met you. I hope you and Zack will be very happy together." Laura Wimberly's voice was soft and musical. She smiled on Camille and Zack with a sincere sweetness that wrenched Camille's heart. Was this the married woman that Zack had told her Rick was having an affair with? Somehow, these two young people didn't fit such a tawdry image.

Laura raised her eyes to Rick's, and Camille's speculation that they were truly in love was confirmed when Rick returned her tender expression. He gazed lovingly down at Laura, who barely reached the middle of his chest.

"How is Mr. Wimberly, Laura?" Zack's question was quiet and kind and full of . . . what? Pity?

"He's not doing too well. I . . . he needed some things so Rick met . . . he offered to bring me out here," she stammered in a whisper and hung her head, unable to meet anyone's eyes.

Rick's arm stole around her shoulders, and she leaned against him. "I guess we'd better get on with our errands. Her . . . Mr. Wimberly will be expecting her back soon. Congratulations again, Zack. Camille." Rick nodded to both of them, and, after Laura said a shy good-bye, they walked away together.

Zack steered Camille toward an arbor away from the main flow of traffic and seated her on a vacant bench. He leaned forward and supported his elbows on his knees, studying his hands clasped between them.

He cleared his throat. "I'm ashamed of myself. I need to make the situation clear. Earlier today I told you that Rick was having an affair with a married woman. I intentionally made it sound ugly. I was being unfair to both him and Laura." He sighed and rubbed his palms briskly up and down his thighs. "In the first place, I doubt that Rick O'Malley would sleep with another man's wife, no matter how much he loved her. And in the second place, I know Laura would never commit adultery."

Camille was uneasy. She had never seen Zack truly apologize for anything. This was a new side of him. "Tell me about them. If it's not confidential."

"Hell, it's not confidential. In that, I was being honest with you. Their story keeps the town gossips supplied with new material." He drew a deep breath and stared off into space as he began. "Rick and Laura started dating when they were in junior high school, and it was one of those romances that lasts forever. They never dated anyone else. They were an institution. It was assumed that when they graduated, they would get married. Laura's family was . . . well, there is no nice word to describe them. They were trash. It's a miracle that Laura is what she is. Anyway, her old man sold her to Jesse Wimberly. I think that old bastard gave her father a thousand dollars for her." At Camille's appalled gasp, Zack continued, "Yeah, incredible, isn't it? In this, the twentieth century. This Wimberly is a reprobate, a former bootlegger, and older than any father. It hasn't been easy for her. There are all kinds of horror stories about the way he treats her. He's even worse than the family was.

"When she got married, Rick enlisted in the Army and volunteered for duty in Vietnam. He tried every way possible to get himself killed. He was awarded every medal for bravery—or stupidity. But in spite of himself, he lived and finally came home. I think you can figure out the rest."

"But why doesn't she just leave Wimberly? She and Rick belong together!"

Zack was taken aback by her vehemence, but he answered calmly. "Old Man Wimberly is sick. She'd never leave him, despite what he's done to her. Besides, she knows how much Rick's religion means to him. She wouldn't burden him with the guilt of taking another man's wife even if she could get a divorce. She encourages Rick to see other women, and he does occasionally, but everyone knows where his heart is. The best they can hope for is that that old geezer will die soon. I hear he's bedridden now."

"That's a terrible way to think, but I can't help but hope that it will happen. They seemed so much in love with each other."

"Are you upset? Were you becoming . . . attached to him?"

"Oh, Zack!" She was exasperated. "Of course not! I like him, and he's great fun. Even through his clowning, though, I saw that he was sad."

"Yeah. I think he overcompensates by being a cutup."

"It's so tragic," Camille murmured. Secretly, she was jealous of the obvious love Rick had for Laura. Zack would never look at her with such warmth and affection.

"I take it that your date with Rick is off for tonight?" Zack asked the question lightly, and Camille joined his laughter.

"Yes, I guess it is," she answered as they walked down the broad, brightly lit aisles of the mall.

"What did you need, Camille?"

For the life of her, she couldn't remember what she had been going to shop for. It had been an unnerving afternoon. "It . . . I . . . some clothes," she stammered.

"Okay." He took her arm and led her to one of the best ladies' shops in the mall. When she demurred, he said gently, "You're not on a working girl's budget anymore, Camille. If *I* think you can afford it, you can."

Under the careful, experienced advice of the gracious saleswoman, Camille tried on several sportswear outfits. She was conscious of Zack's detached inspection as the woman suggested that she model each ensemble for him. She selected a navy wool blazer, camel skirt, and ivory crepe shirt.

"I think I'll take this, Zack. It's practical and easy to wear." She had been shocked at the price tags, which she had conscientiously, though secretly, checked.

He nodded his approval, but asked, "Didn't you like the yellow skirt and sweater?"

"Yes, they were lovely, but—"

"And the green pantsuit with that shiny . . . silk? . . . blouse?"

"Well, yes, I like them all, but—"

"Did they fit you?"

"They fit her beautifully. She's a perfect eight," the saleswoman interjected, beginning to anticipate a larger sale.

"We'll take them all then," Zack told her, ignoring Camille's astonished look. "Have everything pressed and delivered to Bridal Wreath."

"Yes, of course. You must be Mr. Prescott! I've read about you in the society pages."

Zack looked annoyed but said, "This is my wife—"

"So, you and Mrs. Hazelett finally married!"

Camille blushed to the roots of her hair and Zack's face was lived with anger as he answered the woman in cold level tones. "No. This is my wife, the former Camille Jameson of Atlanta. We'll expect the clothes the first thing Monday morning or cancel the purchase."

The saleswoman was aghast at her mistake and tried desperately to make amends. "Surely, Mr. Prescott. I'll . . . We'll . . . I'm happy to have your beautiful wife shopping in my store. Her taste is excellent. We'll send a bill with the clothes. No need to worry about it now."

"Thank you. Camille, I'll wait outside while you're changing."

After she had changed and thanked the flustered saleswoman once again, she left the shop and spotted Zack standing beside one of the fountains in the center of the mall. He had one foot propped up on the low wall of the pool, his hands crossed over the raised knee. He was talking and laughing with two young girls. One of them was a dazzling blonde with big bosoms shamelessly displayed under a tight pink sweater. Camille flushed hotly with jealousy. Zack was reacting with obvious appreciation for the girl's endowments. He saw Camille out of the corner of his eye, and, saying good-bye to the girls, walked over to take her arm.

They had taken only a few steps when Camille said scathingly, "I see that you managed to amuse yourself while you were waiting for me. I've never understood why men find such vulgar women attractive."

He threw back his head and laughed lustily, squeezing her arm. "Jealous already? Here we've been married only a few hours and you sound like a shrewish wife."

His amusement made her even angrier. "Well, if you must flirt, you could at least choose someone closer to your own age! They were hardly more than girls."

He laughed again even harder. "I've known those women for most of their lives, and the one with the breast is older than you, dear heart."

"Oh," Camille replied, embarrassed and refusing to meet his eyes, which were twinkling with humor.

It had grown dark while they were in the mall, and, as they traversed the parking lot toward the car, Camille's stomach growled loudly with hunger.

"I guess I'm going to have to feed you before you cave in," chuckled Zack and, reaching inside her jacket, placed his hand over her stomach just below her breasts. Camille came to an abrupt halt when his fingers moved against the silkiness of her shirt. His other arm was draped across her shoulders and, as they stopped walking, he drew her closer against him. "If we weren't in such a public place, I'd touch you in other places, Camille. You tempt me sorely." He whispered the words against her ear and kissed it lightly before removing his hand and propelling her the rest of the way to the car. She crumpled into the front seat. Her legs had seemingly turned to gelatin.

Zack had chosen The Side Track restaurant for them to take dinner in. It was an old converted railroad building sitting virtually on the train tracks. They enjoyed a sumptuous meal of steaks and baked potatoes after an appetizer of fried zucchini sprinkled with seasonings and grated parmesan cheese. Zack ordered a bottle of wine with dinner, and Camille was feeling a warm glow from the food, the wine, and the man—her husband—across the table from her. He talked her into an ice cream dessert with liqueur and almonds on top of it.

"I won't be able to get into my new clothes if I eat like this all the time," she exclaimed as the aproned waiter set the concoction before her.

Zack smiled at her warmly as he leaned back negligently in his chair and sipped his coffee. She returned his smile then said slowly, "Zack, I want to thank you for the clothes. They're lovely. You shouldn't—"

"Camille, you're my wife now. You obtained that title in an unorthodox manner, I'll grant you, but you are just the same. Any material thing I have belongs to you now. I want you to remember that and take advantage of it." He leaned forward with his elbows on the table. He lowered his voice as his azure eyes searched her face in the candle-light. "Camille, I want you to know—"

"Since when do you take the hired help out on the town, Zack?"

Camille and Zack turned at the same time to see Erica Hazelett standing next to the table. They had been so engrossed in each other, they hadn't seen her come in. She stood beside them in her model's pose, dressed in a soft jersey dress of blue that caressed her slim frame and made her ice-blue eyes seem even more frigid. She lay a possessive hand on Zack's shoulder, and Camille bristled with anger. Hired help indeed!

"Hello, Erica." Zack didn't stand up for her but looked up into her face, which, in the reflected candlelight, was beautiful. Camille watched the two of them with a sinking heart. Why did she have to show up here and now, reminding Zack of how he had been forced to marry someone he felt only contempt for when this was the woman he truly loved? And what had he been about to say when Erica interrupted? She was always making an appearance at the wrong time.

"You've met Camille, I believe," Zack said while Erica's hand moved across his shoulders in leisurely exploration.

"Yes. Hi, Camille," she said a shade ungra-ciously.

"Erica," Camille returned.

Just then an average-looking middle-aged man

joined Erica, and she introduced him as a business associate of her late husband's who was in Natchez to consult with her on some business-related matters. Camille didn't catch all of his name, for Erica made the obligatory introductions with blatant disinterest in her escort.

"You haven't answered my question, Zack. Since when do you take your employees out to dinner?" Erica's beauty was marred as her mouth curled into a sneer when she looked at Camille.

"Camille is no longer just our decorator, Erica. She's my wife. We were married this afternoon." Zack's tone was expressionless, and Camille felt a momentary pang of pity for him. It must be terrible to be stuck with an unwanted wife and forced to present her to the woman you loved.

Erica's eyes turned even colder as they glinted in the candlelight. "You must be joking," she scoffed.

"No. I'm not joking," Zack snapped.

Erica removed her hand from Zack's shoulder as if it had been burned. Then she turned her icy eyes on Camille, eyes full of pure hatred. Camille could almost feel the pinpoints of light that were Erica's eyes stab into her flesh, and she hated herself for cringing under the malevolent state.

Erica whipped her face back to Zack and asked him harshly, "What happened? Were you careless and got her pregnant?"

Camille uttered a small cry of indignation and

protest as she stood, grabbing her purse and coat. To her surprise Zack stood and came around the table to take her arm. They brushed past the other couple, Erica's escort viewing the entire scene with awe, his mouth slack in shock at Erica's incredibly bad manners and lack of decorum.

They hurried past, but Erica grabbed Zack's elbow and spun him around to face her. Since he had such a firm grip on Camille's arm, she had no choice but to stop as well.

"What in the hell do you think you're doing, Zack? I know you didn't marry her for love because you love me. Does this change anything between us? Do you still feel the same way toward me?" Erica's voice was hard, but Camille noted a pleading quality in it, too.

Zack stood looking at her for long moments while Camille prayed she would die on the spot and not have to hear his answer. Finally he said, "No, Erica, this doesn't change in the least the way I feel about you." Then he turned abruptly and practically dragged Camille to his car.

Her emotions were shattered. Her heart and pride lay in tatters somewhere in the depths of her being. A crushing weight was pressing tightly on her lungs, making it almost impossible to breathe. She had stood by while her husband of a few hours had all but declared his love for another woman. Why hadn't she stopped the ceremony this afternoon? Surely Rayburn wouldn't prefer that his son and she, whom she knew Rayburn had come to have a high regard for, suffer in a loveless marriage. Why hadn't Zack stopped the charade before it went any further? She would have been mortified, yes, but was this any better? Could she stand to be constantly humiliated knowing that her husband loved Erica Hazelett but had been all but forced to marry her?

The worst part of it was that she loved him. Every fiber of her being cried out to him to love her back, but she knew that to hope he might grow to love her was a futile wish. He would forever blame her for trapping him into a marriage he never would have wanted.

She raised a clenched fist to stifle the sobs that erupted out of her mouth as they drove through the darkened streets of Natchez toward Bridal Wreath. What awaited her there, at the hands of her new husband, she had no idea.

Ten

*C*amille tried unsuccessfully to tie the shoulder straps of her nightgown. Her fingers were trembling in such a way that the task proved to be nearly impossible. She was standing before a dressing table she had never seen, looking into a cheval glass that reflected a room she had never been in, belonging to a man who was an enigma to her.

When Zack had parked the car in the garage of Bridal Wreath, he turned to her and said unemotionally, "Dearly and Simon are very excited about all of this. They've come to like you, consider you a member of the family. They know nothing of what my father learned about. To them we are a happy, loving couple who have restrained our love and now can share it openly. Let's not disappoint them. Keep up the act."

He ushered her into the house where Dearly and Simon greeted them with warm and hearty congratulations. Camille hated deceiving them, hated deceiving everyone, but she, like Zack, was powerless to prevent this catalytic chain of events. The couple assured her that all of her things had been moved into Zack's room, but she could rearrange them as she saw fit. Dearly was smiling sweetly at both her and Zack, and Simon's dark eyes and white teeth were gleaming in his kind face. Impulsively Camille went to each of them and hugged them in turn. In their innocence of the true situation, she looked upon them as a lifeline to sanity and reality.

Zack escorted her upstairs after the Mitchells retired to their own apartment over the garage. He opened the door of his bedroom and stood aside for her to enter. To her surprise he didn't follow her in. Instead he said, "I'll be back shortly," and turned away to go back down the stairs.

The room was masculine, the furniture massive. Camille was pleased to see a large fireplace in one wall with a cheerful fire burning in the grate. It must be connected to the same chimney as the fireplace in the parlor, she surmised, remembering the placement of the rooms. There was the pervading scent of Zack's cologne in the air despite the fragrant flowers that had been delivered by the wedding caterer and arranged attractively around the room.

The king size bed dominated one wall. Rather than having a standard headboard, the bed was flanked by book shelves. Between the loaded and somewhat cluttered shelves were hung stunning graphics, each framed in a narrow brass frame. The bedspread, which was already turned down, was an austere stripe in shades of brown, beige, and blue. Zack had good taste.

Crossing to the closet and opening it, she saw that all of her clothes were hanging with Zack's. Several cowboy hats were standing side by side on the shelves of the closet. On another shelf, boots and shoes were arranged in rows. All the clothes were hung in groups—dress slacks, dress shirts, sport coats, suit coats, jeans, and so on. *No one can accuse Zack of being sloppy,* she mused.

She had found her lingerie arranged neatly in drawers after pulling out several full of socks, handkerchiefs, and masculine underwear.

She went through the door leading into the bathroom and saw that it was large and modern and masculine in decor, having brown and beige striped towels hanging on the brass racks. Dark blue was the accent color in the rug, tiles, and other appointments in the room. She recognized several pieces of Zack's gold jewelry in a glass dish near the marble basin. A tortoise shell comb, a brush, several bottles of cologne and after-shave lotion were all poignant reminders that the room belonged to Zack.

She found her own toiletries on the other side of the dressing table and soon had the long, deep, chocolate brown tub filled with warm, bubbly

190

water. She took a leisurely bath, hoping that the warm, caressing water would dispel some of her anxiety over the immediate future.

She noticed the gift-wrapped box on the bed as she came out of the bathroom after brushing her hair and cleaning her teeth. The negligee was nestled in crackling tissue paper along with a loving note from her mother.

Now she stood before the mirror, the sheer, silky green fabric swirling around her as she tried to tie the bows that held the gown on either shoulder. It hung loose and open except for another pair of satin ribbons that tied the front and back panels together at the waist. She was dismayed at her reflection. The negligee was so chaste from the front and back, but alarmingly alluring from the sides, and the fabric was much more sheer than she had first thought. Should she put it back in the box and choose another nightgown, one more tailored? No, her mother would surely ask her if she had liked it, and she hated to pile other lies on top of the lie she was living. Besides, why was she so nervous? She had no idea what Zack was going to do. Would he expect her to share this bed with him tonight, or would he move her into the room on the other side of the bathroom?

Before she could speculate any further, she heard the door open and she whirled around to see Zack framed in the jamb. The firelight picked up the blond streaks in his hair and gave his skin a golden glow. He looked exactly the way he had in Utah. She moaned softly at the thought, but it came out sounding more like a whimper. They stood for several moments looking at each other across the space of the room, then Zack asked softly, "Are you finished in the bathroom?"

She couldn't answer around the nervous lump in her throat, so she merely nodded. He crossed to the closet and took off his sport coat and hung it up neatly. His belt came off next, and he hung it on a metal rack on the inside of the door. He leaned down and pulled a boot jack from the closet floor, then, placing his heels against it one at a time, tugged off his boots. These he placed on the top shelf and returned the boot jack to its accustomed position. Every movement was unhurried, meticulous, and practiced. Camille watched warily as he went to a bureau and took something out of a drawer before going into the bathroom and closing the door.

She listened to the water splashing, the opening and closing of drawers, the rustle of clothing, and wondered what she was going to say when Zack came back into the bedroom. This marriage was a travesty, a mockery. They had both been forced into it. Neither wanted it. For though she loved Zack with all her heart and soul, she knew that he didn't love her, and she wasn't going to submit to his lovemaking when love wasn't the motivating force. Sex should be a personal and intimate commitment between two people who loved each other. What had happened in Utah had been a mistake she had regretted ever since. She refused to fall into the trap again. She had disdained her physical weakness for two years now, and she wasn't going to spend the rest of her life acting out a farce.

She would reason with Zack that they could stay married—without being intimate—until Rayburn was well and could take the disappointment of them separating. She was certain that Zack would go along with her plan. After all, he would be eager to get back to Erica, wouldn't he? The dress shop owner's assumption that Zack's new wife was Erica Hazelett must mean that there had been rumors of a pending marriage between them. She would reiterate these facts when he came to her.

But what if he had other ideas? Suppose he forced his connubial rights on her? What if he ravished her? No, not Zack. That was not his style. He was a reasonable man, and she would play to his pragmatic nature. They could continue being good friends, companions making the best of a bad situation, and nothing more.

She felt much better after having decided what course of action she would take. She crossed the room and stood facing the fireplace, not knowing that her figure was silhouetted against its flames. That was the first thing Zack saw as he came out of the bathroom and switched off the light behind him.

Camille knew that he was in the room with her, and all of her recent resolves vanished into vapor. They were replaced by trembling anticipation as she heard him come up behind her.

What was wrong with her? Why didn't she turn around and face him and have the big showdown she had plotted so carefully? Instead, every muscle of her body had turned to water as she caught the scent of his soap and cologne along with the male muskiness that he exuded.

"I like you in that color, Camille. It complements your unusual complexion." Did she imagine that feather-light kiss on her bare shoulder? "You should only stand in sunlight or firelight because they burnish your hair with beautiful highlights." He gathered her thick, curly hair in a gentle fist, lifted it off her neck, and pressed a kiss into her nape. She sighed in spite of herself, against her will, and swayed against him, the solid wall of his chest supporting her back. He clasped her waist with both hands and stirred the soft fabric of the nightgown against her skin as his face nuzzled her hair, her neck, behind her ears.

"Camille, Camille," he breathed as he moved one hand to her abdomen and drew her against him so she could feel the strength of his desire. He cupped one breast in his warm hand and moaned huskily in her ear as he explored its soft curve.

He turned her gently to face him, and she was startled to see that his chest was bare. He was wearing pajama bottoms tied carelessly below his navel. The hair that spread like a fan on the upper part of his chest tapered to a silky golden line that disappeared into the waistband of the pajamas. His mother's cross, suspended from the gold chain, lay on the crisp curls. His masculine appeal was heart-stopping.

She met his eyes and read the desire that fired them. Desire, nothing else. Surely not love. But she was powerless to obey her instinctive common sense and push away from him. Even as she opened her mouth to speak what she knew should be said, he closed his lips over it and sealed her words inside. His mouth was delicious, tasting of the toothpaste he had just used, and she drank of its nectar. His tongue met hers and moved against her lips, her teeth, and searched her mouth in a tantalizing quest.

"I've waited so long to have you again, Camille. Don't make me wait any longer," he pleaded as he buried his face in the hollow of her throat. She felt his hands working with the ribbons on her shoulders. The gown fell to her feet, forming a pool of silk on the carpet. He cupped her face with both his hands and gazed into the amber lights of her eyes. His eyes devoured her body, his hands following, touching everywhere his eyes roamed.

Her mind screamed *no,* but her body was beyond the limits of restraint. She was quivering with desire for him, for the fulfillment his body promised hers. Every nerve cell was singing, harmonizing with his, building to a crescendo of emotion. *Not this way! Not without his love,* her conscience told her, but even as it did, unwillingly, her arms went of their own accord and locked behind his head.

He clutched her to him. She met his fiery kisses with an internal flame of her own. Her breasts were flattened against the hardness of his chest, the soft golden down that covered it teasing her nipples to peaks of desire. When Zack's stroking fingers failed to assuage them, he used his mouth. His tongue eagerly traced the pattern of their arousal. But there was no appeasement. They cried out with the rest of her body for more . . . more.

He raised his head and groaned into her hair, "Oh, Camille, I hurt. Heal me."

She kicked away the forsaken nightgown as he lifted her and carried her to the bed, depositing her gently on the pillows before stepping out of the pajamas that hugged his loins.

His body covered hers. His gentle hands and seeking lips brought her to a fevered pitch of longing. She welcomed his weight, was thrilled by the contrasts of their bodies.

It all came back to her. All that she had tried to forget, forced herself to negate as a dream, a fantasy, came flooding back now in the glory of Zack's body fusing with hers. It was a homecoming, a recognition of fulfillment, of belonging, a meeting of kindred spirits. This recognition had frightened a younger, more innocent girl two years ago, and she had run from it. This time there was no running away. This time Camille surrendered to it. Now she grasped it, embraced it. *Now, now!* even as their bodies exploded with the intense heat of passion and melted together in absolute gratification.

Camille stood at the cheval glass brushing her hair. She studied herself critically. She looked no different except for an apricot flush on her cheeks, which she attributed to the fire in the grate she had just rekindled and not to the memory of last evening in Zack's bed. Their hunger for each other had been insatiable and they had not been denied. Their night together in Utah paled in comparison to the shared bliss of last night.

She stifled the sob that rose in her throat. In the light of day, she realized that nothing had changed. He still didn't love her. Why did her body betray her so? She wanted to hate him, to loathe him, but every time she so much as thought of his hands and lips and how they played her body like a finely tuned instrument, she became aflame with desire for his touch, his caress, his kiss.

The shower in the bathroom stopped running

and she braced herself for the inevitable moment when she would have to face Zack. He had already gone into the bathroom before she awakened. She had quickly left the comfortable warmth of the bed and hurriedly wrapped herself in a dressing gown that wasn't sheer or revealing in cut. She wanted to put every barrier she could between her and her husband. Vulnerability was to be avoided. She couldn't afford it.

The bathroom door opened and Zack stepped through it, vigorously drying his hair with a towel. He had a terrycloth wrapper tucked around his slim, taut hips. Otherwise, his body was disturbingly exposed to her, and Camille's heart skipped erratically at the sight.

"Good morning. You didn't have to get up just because I did." He was cheerful, his eyes sparkling blue, as he crossed to her, draping the towel around the strong column of his neck. The damp hair clung to his head in a boyish, charming manner and his brilliant smile was beguiling. Why couldn't he be fat and ugly and bald? Then maybe she could despise him as she should.

"You look beautiful this morning, Camille," he whispered as he placed his hands on her shoulders and drew her against him. She resisted surrender as his lips traced a tender path across her temple, down her cheek, and finally came to rest on her mouth, claiming it with a burning kiss. Her whole body went rigid as she fought the tremors of longing that were already shaking her control. His probing tongue encountered sealed lips where hours before it had found eager acquiescence and equal desire.

He didn't countenance her resistance, and his hands became more demanding, his lips more per-suasive. She parted her lips in an effort to object to his ardor, but he used that instant to find what he was seeking, and the touch of his tongue on hers ignited once again the fires of passion she was struggling to quench.

In spite of her anger toward him for the power he wielded over her and berating herself for her weakness to it, she moaned pleasurably as he placed one hand on the small of her back and drew her closer to his hard body. He found the opening to her dressing gown and slipped one hand inside, fondling her breast gently as his lips moved down her throat to the top swelling curve. "You're love-ly, Camille. Soft, beautiful, feminine," he whis-pered as he brushed butterfly kisses on her smooth flesh. "Your body satisfies mine completely."

That was still all it was to him! It was purely a physical attraction. Yes, their bodies had recog-nized this chemistry between them right away, but there should be more. There must be more! She loved his body, and it was useless to deny that, but she loved him for so many other reasons. It was his total lack of love for her which wounded her, pierced her spirit. *He loves someone else even as he uses me to satisfy his sexual lust. No. No!*

The anguished tears that had been threatening since the extraordinary wedding ceremony yesterday finally surfaced, and Camille's body shook with a different kind of tremor that Zack was sensitive to immediately. He raised his head and impaled her with his eyes. Tenderly, his fingers traced the trail of her tears before he brushed them away.

"What is it, Camille?" His tone was soft, but she could see the smallest flicker of anger in his eyes and a muscle in his jaw twitched, a trait Camille had come to recognize as a sign of extreme agitation and impatience.

She stammered and lowered her lashes in order to avoid meeting those penetrating eyes. "I . . . please don't make . . . love . . . to me again. I can't. I'm sorry." And she was. Far sorrier than he could ever guess. Even as she denied him, she longed to know again the wonder of lying in the security of his arms.

He stepped back from her, relinquishing his hold. Camille quickly covered her exposed breasts, a gesture he watched with derision and obvious disgust.

"Is it to terrible, my lovemaking, that my bride of less than twenty-four hours cringes and weeps when I touch her?" he asked scornfully, his lip twisted into a sneer.

No! her mind screamed. *If only you knew how*

much I crave your touch! Instead she said with a cracking voice, "No, Zack, it has nothing to do with that. You should know by now that I respond—" She broke off, unable to continue under the implacable blue stare.

"Then what, Camille? What!?" His frustration was apparent.

She twisted her hands and clamped her teeth over her bottom lip to keep it from trembling. *I love you. I love you.* Why couldn't she tell him? Perhaps then he would take her in his arms and pledge his undying love for her. She couldn't; he wouldn't. He had loved once. Dearly had told her so. Whoever that woman was had hurt him deeply, and he hadn't been ready to love again until he gave his love to Erica. Now he had been forced to forfeit that.

Camille was in an untenable predicament. Without revealing her love for him, how was she going to explain her torment? She couldn't allow him to see her true feelings. It would be too humiliating, and he would regard her with more contempt than ever before.

"I . . . We . . . At Snow Bird—"

"Dammit, woman, are you never going to forgive me for that?" He smacked his palms together smartly and she jumped. "How long must I be punished before it's sufficient? We're married now. What more could I do to redeem myself with you?"

Punishment! This marriage was punishment to him. Somewhere in a quiet, private spot of her heart, she had held on to a thread of hope that he might not view it as such, but his words had dashed that hope. A tight pain was squeezing her chest, and a burning flush of shame swept her body. Zack flung the towel from around his neck and into a nearby chair, slammed one clenched fist into the palm of his other hand, and then faced her belligerently, hands on his hips.

It was his arrogant stance and expression of righteous indignation that snapped Camille from shame and humility to fury. He was blaming her again! Just as always, she saw accusation in his frigid eyes.

"Don't get angry with *me,* Mr. Prescott. This whole obscene situation is your fault. It was you who took my innocence without so much as a thought—"

"How in the hell do you know what I thought?" he interrupted. "You have no idea what I was thinking, do you? You ran away, remember. I never had a chance to tell you what I was thinking."

"Then tell me now. What were you thinking that night when you so peacefully and inculpably fell asleep beside me?" she shouted back at him. He was momentarily shaken by her flare of anger, but he recovered himself quickly, pulling that impenetrable mask over his features.

A short expulsion of breath escaped the grim

lips, and he raked tense fingers through his drying hair before answering resignedly, "I don't know what I was thinking, Camille." He spread his arms palms up in mute appeal. "I am a single adult male. I met an attractive woman—girl. I enjoyed her company for several days, then shared what I thought was a mutually satisfying physical experience." He shrugged almost apologetically. "I don't know what else you want me to say."

I want you to say that you fell in love with me, she grieved silently. She sniffed back more tears and asked, "You thought of nothing else?"

"Yes! Hell, yes. I thought you were highly intelligent. I thought you were amusing, fun to be with. Surely you know I thought—think—you were beautiful and incredibly sexy. I liked your hair and the golden lights in your eyes." His voice grew husky. "I liked the look and feel of your breasts and the taste of your mouth." He took a tentative step toward her, but when she reacted by stepping backward, he continued with no inflection. "If you want me to say that I planned a glorious future for us in those few hours, I'm sorry. I didn't think up names for our first three children. Do you condemn me for following through with an instinct as old as time, Camille? A man and a woman meet, and they are attracted to each other, and they have sex together. It happens all the time."

She bowed her head and mumbled, "Not to me, it doesn't." He didn't respond to that. The room was silent except for the logs popping in the fire-place. Far away, Camille heard Dearly rattling pans in the kitchen and Simon's low, modulated voice. Tears rolled unchecked down Camille's cheeks. There was no reason to hide them now.

Finally Zack spoke quietly. "I know it doesn't, Camille. The fact that I was the first . . . the only . . . believe me, it was a surprise. And it makes you special. But do you censure the rest of the population? Do you expect mere humans to live by your standards?" There was the slightest trace of humor in his words, but Camille met his eyes unwaveringly.

"No, Zack, no!" she groaned pleadingly. "Please don't think of me as a pious prude. But *I* have to live by my standards. I know what's right and wrong for *me*. And without—" She bit off the word "love" and hurriedly lowered her gaze from the blue eyes that had become remarkably tender.

He came to her quickly and softly. His voice was a hoarse whisper when he asked, "Why did you run away from me Camille?" He put his index finger under her chin and raised it so she was forced to meet his eyes.

How would he react if she told him the truth? What would he do if she said, "Because I knew even then that I was falling in love with you. You possessed my heart and soul just as surely as you possessed my body, and I realized that no other man would ever do that. I panicked at the thought that you would reject me. I couldn't stand the thought of your leaving me once I had found you, so I spared myself that by leaving you first." She couldn't make such an admission. She must hold onto one particle of pride. She would convince him that it was something else and find protection in that.

She licked her lips and began, "I told you that it was wrong for me. I felt guilty—"

"Oh, God, no!" he cursed. "Are we back to 'ruined, cheap, and dirty'? Well, I certainly don't want to be responsible for a stupid, self-destructive attitude like that," he sneered caustically. "You may rest assured, Mrs. Prescott, that your husband will demand nothing physical from you. I wouldn't touch you now if you were the last woman in the world. Rest easy, dear wife, that I won't subject you to my uncouth, base, lustful, and degrading invasion of your chaste body again."

She was stunned by the vehemence of his bitterness. As Camille stood mutely in the center of the room, he went to the closet and grabbed a pair of jeans, then crossed to the bureau and jerked open one of the drawers. He cursed expansively as it opened to its full extent, spilling some of her lacy undergarments onto the floor. He finally located the drawer containing his underwear and, extracting a pair, slammed the drawer shut.

Before he went out of the room, he stopped and said smoothly, with surprising calm that sounded more deadly than shouting, "You can move your things into the other bedroom. This is my room, and, as long as you aren't going to be under the covers, I don't want you to be underfoot either."

With a contemptuous leer, he whipped the terry wrapper from around his waist and flung the scrap of material to her feet. He stood there before her brazenly exposing her to his nakedness before he stamped out of the room carrying his clothes.

Camille stumbled to the bed and collapsed upon it, sobbing into the pillow that was fragrant with Zack's scent.

Eleven

*B*reakfast that morning set a precedent for each morning thereafter. Camille and Zack sat across the table from each other barely able to conceal their hostility. They spoke politely about inconsequential topics. Camille knew that Dearly and Simon were dismayed at the strange attitude of the new bride and groom toward each other. She and Zack didn't fool them.

This time of year wasn't a busy season for the plantation, and the routine chores could have been handled by Zack's employees there, but he left early every day and returned late in the evenings. He answered Camille's courteous questions in monosyllables, but she gathered that he was devoting most of his time to horse breeding. He never went out in the evenings, but retired early to his room with a book or watched television in what was now referred to as "Rayburn's den."

Camille wasted no time in moving her things to the bedroom that comprised the other half of the master suite. It was a comfortable room, though not as large as Zack's. There was no fireplace. The furniture was rosewood and graceful in design, much like that in the dowager house.

Her mother telephoned often. Once she asked if she should send the rest of Camille's things to Natchez. Camille always tried to sound cheerful and give the impression that she and Zack were deliriously happy, but she hedged on her mother's sending anything else to her. Wasn't this only a temporary arrangement? Was she ready to accept it as such? She must. However, she told her mother that she and Zack were planning a trip to Atlanta soon, and she would decide then what to throw away, give away, or bring back with her. It was a feasible lie, and her mother didn't suspect her true reason for not wanting any more of her belongings at Bridal Wreath. The less she had to move out when she left for good, the better.

While Zack filled his days with work at the plantation, she continued working on the restoration of the house with fanatic zeal. She relaxed a little bit when Rayburn's new suite of rooms was completed. The rest of the house was all but finished, lacking only the final artistic touches. A few pieces of furniture had yet to be reupholstered, but she could now begin the fun part of arranging silk flowers, rehanging portraits and other pictures and mirrors, rearranging bric-a-brac, and choosing the other appointments of each room with utmost care.

Zack had never again referred to the color in the dining room that he had found so offensive. The room had turned out to be beautiful, just as Camille had planned that it would. The contrasts between light and dark and pastel blended so well that one didn't notice them. One only saw a gorgeous, serene room. But if Zack had given attention to the results of her hard work, he didn't comment on it to her.

She carried through the Southern theme wherever she could, using silk dogwood blossoms in one arrangement in the parlor and real cotton bolls still attached to their dried stalks to fill a tall, crystal vase on a table in the entrance hall.

While she arranged the latter, she had the strong urge to submit to the tears gathering behind her lids. She had come to love this house, and it was going to be painful to leave it once it was finished and Rayburn was home and in good enough health to tell him about her and Zack's separation.

Any former job she had undertaken had been just that—a job. No matter how satisfied she was with the finished product, and even if the customer shared similar taste with her, she was always ready to leave the project at its completion and accept the challenge of another. Why was she so attached to Bridal Wreath? Was it because she was in love with the owner?

She gazed out the front door to the broad expanse of lawn. Zack had surprised her by hiring gardeners to do remedial work on the trees and shrubs. They had been pruned and fertilized. The flowerbeds had been weeded, and new bulbs had been planted. In the spring, the front lawn would be as lovely as Rayburn's backyard. Gone was the aura of neglect and disrepair that Bridal Wreath had radiated when Camille arrived several months earlier. She sighed. Were there never to be any happy, laughing children to play on those lovely yards?

How she wished that things could have been different. If only she and Zack could live here happily in this gorgeous house and raise a family to carry on the traditions. But it wasn't to be.

Living with Zack Prescott these days was like living with a stranger. When their eyes happened to meet, his were cold, indifferent, implacable. She could hear him lock her bathroom door whenever he went in there from his bedroom. She would listen to the splashing water and imagine him standing before the basin shaving, the terry cloth wrapper snug around his hips. If he minded or even noticed her makeup, hair curlers, and other feminine implements in his bathroom, he made no mention of it. Only once, when she was soaking in the bathtub, did she hear him try the door from his bedroom. When he discovered that it was locked, he said nothing. She heard him turn away, and he didn't try the door again while she was there.

The tension in the house was almost palpable,

but the hardest times to endure were their hospital visits to Rayburn. Camille and Zack would drive together, usually in complete silence. When they arrived at the hospital, they would put on their happy faces, like actors of Greek theater putting on masks. They acted out their parts, playing to their audience of one, presenting him with the image of a happily wedded couple. They had never talked about their charade, it just came about with both of them understanding that it was crucial to Rayburn's health that nothing at this point should agitate him.

The second week of November, Dr. Daniels told them that his patient could come home by the end of the week. Plans for Rayburn's homecoming overshadowed everything else. Even Zack refrained from going to the plantation in order to help make everything ready in time. He and Simon filled the den-conservatory with plants until Zack grumbled that if they ever needed money, they could open a nursery. Dearly planned meals around Dr. Daniels's strict diet for Rayburn and improvised how she could change the bland and tasteless food into dishes more appetizing in an effort to keep Rayburn within his restrictions. Camille was anxious about his liking his new rooms. She checked every detail and rearranged the furniture a dozen times before she was satisfied.

Her relationship with Zack weighed heavy on her mind. Dearly and Simon were too polite to comment on it, though she knew they sensed the tension. And, of course, they knew she had moved to the other bedroom and that she and her husband didn't sleep together. Now that Rayburn would be on the first floor and forbidden to climb the stairs, he wouldn't know about that. At least not right away. But could she keep up this tormenting play-acting at home as she did for an hour at the hospital? When they would walk through the corridors of the hospital, his thigh would press against hers. As they stood together at Rayburn's bedside, Zack often draped an arm across her shoulders or around her waist, drawing her close. He held her hand and stroked his thumb over the pulse in her wrist. He kissed her fingers lightly with warm lips before relinquishing her hand. Once his fingers had trailed up and down her arm in an absentminded caress that made her heart pound. A few times, he had leaned down and brushed a soft kiss on her forehead. His breath stirred the hair at her temples.

She knew these gestures were for her father-in-law's benefit, but she responded to them just the same, and it never failed to leave her with a feeling of self-loathing at her own body's susceptibility. If he continued these tiny ministrations when they were constantly around Rayburn at home, how could she bear it? She longed to fall into Zack's arms and beg him to still the rapid beating of her heart and satisfy the desire that engulfed her even as she denied that it existed.

*   *   *

George Daniels had insisted that he bring Rayburn home in his car so that the family would be able to greet the head of the household properly.

Zack and Camille stood on the new front porch, watching the sleek car drive over the lane that Zack had had resurfaced. As it drew nearer, Zack put a possessive arm around her waist. It must have been her imagination that his fingers deftly brushed the underside of her breast. But why then did her breath catch in her throat, and Zack's body stiffen in a jerking reaction?

Dearly was weeping copiously into her handkerchief as Rayburn mounted the steps and hugged her. He shook hands with Simon and then embraced Camille and Zack together.

"Welcome home, Dad. We're glad to have you back." Zack's voice had a slight hoarseness to it, and Camille knew that he was struggling to hold on to his composure. He loved his father very much. She should know better than anyone to what extent that love went. How many men would marry a woman they detested just to please a parent?

They were all filled with expectancy as they led Rayburn into the house. He stood inside the front door for long moments and stared at the transformation the house had undergone with Camille's supervision. He walked slowly to the opening of each room leading off the entrance hall and gazed in wonder at the restored beauty of the home he loved so much. She saw tears glistening in his eyes as he turned toward her and extended his arms. She went to him without hesitation and returned his warm embrace. Over his shoulder, she surprised Zack in an unguarded moment and met his eyes. They had softened; the lines around his mouth weren't grim and set as they had been since the morning after their wedding. His expression was tender. When he realized that she was looking at him, he shook his head slightly and said quickly, "Dad, Camille has another surprise for you." Whatever she had read in his face a moment before had vanished.

"I don't know if I can stand any more surprises this morning. Camille, it's . . . I . . ." he floundered and then chuckled. "I guess I'm trying to say that it's better than I ever imagined it could be. Thank you, daughter."

She blushed at his flattery. "You helped with the selections, remember, Rayburn." He had insisted that she call him by his given name ever since the wedding. "Come see what else we've done."

She took his elbow and, with the others following, led him toward the rear of the house where the screened porch had been. When Rayburn saw the new den with the window blinds opened to reveal the late autumn landscape outside, the tropical plants dappled by filtered sunlight, and the new furniture mixed with all of his favorite things, he was truly taken aback. He wandered through the new den and then went into the bedroom and accompanying bath. Everyone breathed a collective sigh of relief as he said with a touch of awe, "I love it!"

The rest of the morning was spent settling Rayburn into his new rooms. Even more plants and flowers, his gifts while in the hospital, were moved in, much to Zack's consternation. Dearly and Simon were ever at Rayburn's beck and call, though, just before Dr. Daniels left, he admonished them not to spoil his patient too badly.

Rayburn was reluctant to let Zack and Camille out of his sight. He seemed hungry for the sight and sound of them. They stayed near him all day except for the times that Zack demanded Rayburn take his naps.

Later in the evening while they were all sitting around the new television set watching a fairly recent movie, Rayburn said again, "I love my new rooms. But you can't fool me, Zack. I realize that I've been moved downstairs to insure you and Camille more privacy." He laughed deeply, and it was a good thing that he was so engrossed with the remote control gadget of the television set that he missed the guilty look that passed between Zack and his wife and the hurriedly averted glances of Dearly and Simon.

Camille leaned into the bathroom mirror and applied the finishing strokes of mascara to her eyelashes. The mirror was still a bit foggy from her recent shower, and, since it was so steamy in the room, she wore only a brief pair of bikini panties.

At the instant she returned the mascara to her makeup drawer, the bathroom door from Zack's bedroom opened and he stepped through it. Their eyes locked in mutual astonishment over the expanse of the few feet that separated them.

Camille stood rooted to the floor, flushing hotly and shivering with cold as she watched his eyes fix on her breasts before moving to somewhere in the area of her navel. She checked the ludicrous impulse to cover herself. What good would it do? The damage had already been done, and she would only look foolish.

"Good morning," he said huskily when his eyes finally returned to her face.

"Good morning," she answered, her voice none too steady. He must have just stepped into the worn jeans, faded almost white, for he had still been zipping them as he opened the door. His chest was bare, as were his feet. His hair was still tousled from sleep. He had never looked more devastatingly appealing.

"I . . . uh . . . I should have knocked." Camille was glad he, too, was finding it hard to concentrate. His usual aplomb seemed to have deserted him.

"I thought I had locked your door. I'm sorry." She could barely hear her own words for the loud pounding of her heartbeat reverberating in her head.

"Please don't be on my account." Some of the mocking quality had returned to Zack's voice, and he grinned at her lazily, automatically putting her on guard.

"I was just about to dress," she said defensively. "I'll be out in a minute." She turned her back and began gathering up the clothes that were hung on a decorative wall hook. In the blink of an eye, he was behind her and grabbing the clothes out of her hand.

"What are you doing?" she asked, panicked by his sudden action and whirling to face him.

They were standing so close that her breasts were brushing against the hair on his chest, and she stepped back hurriedly, but not soon enough to prevent a normal physical response from her nipples. Zack saw it and grinned sardonically.

"Well now," he drawled, "since I don't have the pleasure of undressing my wife like most husbands do, maybe I could *dress* her."

"Zack, give me back my clothes! Please." She tried to be stern, but she sounded ridiculous even to herself. Her costume wasn't exactly obedience-provoking. He ignored her and half-leaned, half-sat against the dressing table. Before she could react, he had grasped her around the waist and pulled her toward him, placing her between his long legs.

He rubbed his hands together eagerly and said with irritating relish, "Now, let's see. I guess this goes on next." He held up the scrap of sheer fabric and lace that was her bra.

"Zack, please—"

"Yes, I remember," he leered, "you always wear this kind and for the life of me, I don't know why you bother. Oh, well," he shrugged. His face was no more than an inch from hers as he reached around her and slid her arms into the shoulder straps of the bra. She was drowning in the deep blue pools of his eyes before he straightened and, drawing the sides of the garment together, fastened the clasp under her breasts. "A perfect fit," he murmured. He brushed his fingers across the tops of her breasts, which were still exposed by the demi-cup bra. She shuddered as he glided his hands over the soft mounds of flesh, down her taut stomach, and settled on her waist, drawing her closer to him. He buried his face in the deep cleavage, nibbling gentle kisses with burning lips. "You smell so good," he whispered. "So good." The abrasion of his unshaven jaw against her smooth skin was an unexpected pleasure. He caught one nipple between his lips, and, even encased as it was in a sheer veil of fabric, the moist pull of his mouth caused a sweet, agonizing desire to course through her body. Camille settled her hands on his shoulders as she leaned into him. NO! She caught herself just in time and pushed away from him. "Don't, Zack," she gasped.

"Don't?"

"Yes, please don't." Was she sobbing even though her eyes were dry?

"Okay," he replied cheerfully and released her immediately. She was shocked at his obedience and, if she admitted it, a little disappointed.

He was not to be daunted. "Jeans next, right?" He held up her jeans expectantly, and she had no choice but to support herself with one hand on his shoulder as she stepped first into one leg and then the other. She was acutely aware of his warm breath against her stomach as he leaned down to pull the tight jeans up her legs and over her hips. As he reached to close them, she said quickly, "I'll fasten them," and hurriedly drew up the zipper and snapped the snap. He grinned at her wickedly and shrugged.

"Okay. I'll do the belt." Again his arms went around her as he drew the belt through the loops at the back of her jeans. His head was pressed against her chest, and she noticed that it was taking an unnecessary length of time for such a simple task.

"Zack, you're not fool—"

"There, I've got it now. I was having a little trouble with one of the loops." He lifted his head to meet her eyes. His mouth was curled into such a mischievous grin, and his eyes were dancing with such devilish delight that Camille was tempted to laugh with him and tease back. She stymied the impulse and looked back at him coolly. He was not at all impressed by her hauteur.

"Pretty blouse," he commented as he held it while she put her arms into the sleeves. He buttoned the cuffs with aggravating care. She expected him to do the same with the buttons on the front, but when he looked at her this time, she could see that he had dropped his teasing manner. He held her eyes with his. She couldn't escape the hypnotic pull they had over her senses. He slipped his hands into the open shirt and pressed them onto her breasts. Having a will of its own, her body began to respond. She leaned nearer to him, and one of his hands closed around the back of her neck, drawing her face down to meet his.

"Zack—"

"Don't say 'don't.' "

"Zack—"

"Don't say 'don't.' "

And then she couldn't say anything for his mouth was blending with hers. In a heartbeat, he was off the dressing table and standing with her, pulling her into him with a ferocity that was as frightening as it was thrilling. His tongue plundered her mouth hungrily as if he could not get enough of her. Their bodies welded together, and, even through the thickness of their jeans. Camille knew his desire and answered it with an instinctive pressure of her hips.

Finally his lips left her mouth and traveled on a fiery path down her neck to her throat. She clutched his bare back and marveled at the rippling muscles under her fingers. The hair on his chest and stomach tickled her as he pressed her torso against him.

"Camille, please," he moaned. "Why do you refuse what we both want so badly? *Why?*"

The words were ground out near her ear and she recognized the anguish in them. He was suffering through all of this, too. But his suffering was only physical, while hers was of the spirit as well. Oh, she did want him. She wanted him with a passion she never knew she could be capable of. It would be so easy to submit. She longed for release from this painful torment. Release that could only be found in his arms. But she knew that to assuage it would only bring more pain to her soul, and she couldn't do it. It took every ounce of will, every vestige of her strength, to push away from him.

She saw the bafflement, the absolute incomprehension in his eyes, and she almost dismissed her resolve. But then the blue eyes became clouded with mounting frustration that grew into savage anger even as she watched.

"Dammit, Camille! I know you want me as much as I want you." His fingers dug into her shoulders, and he spoke through clenched teeth.

"Let me go, Zack," she screamed. She was on

the verge of hysteria, hating herself for what she must do for both their sakes.

He released her so suddenly that she reeled backward. She allowed herself one fleeting glimpse of his hard, bitter face before she flung herself into her bedroom and slammed the connecting door. She fell against it and slid down its cold surface to the floor. Sobbing uncontrollably she whispered, "I *do* want you, Zack. If only you'd say you love me."

That evening Zack went out alone for the first time since their marriage. Camille couldn't face him at breakfast after what had happened in the bathroom. Dearly brought a tray to her room. After she had eaten some bisquits and drunk several cups of coffee, she felt somewhat restored. She was just leaving her room when she heard the telephone ring. As she passed Zack's bedroom door, she heard him answer it, pause, and then say, "Hello, Erica." His voice was light and happy, a far cry from the harsh, bitter tones he had flung at her an hour before. She didn't want to hear the rest of the conversation, so she hurried down the hall and went downstairs to visit with Rayburn.

The day seemed to drag by. Whenever she and Zack were in the same room, the anger and tension between them was almost tangible, separating them like an impenetrable curtain.

At dinner when he announced that he was going

out for the evening, her heart plummeted. Even though he made some vague excuse to Rayburn about a poker game with friends, she knew that he was more likely meeting Erica. Was this their first meeting since the scene in the restaurant on the day of his wedding, or was this just the first one she knew anything about? Would she have been suspicious of his evening out had she not heard him talking to Erica this morning on the telephone? It struck Camille as strange that Erica would chance calling Zack at home instead of him trying to contact her. Did the woman have no shame? She apparently was confident in Zack's love for her.

Zack stayed out until early the next morning. Camille didn't fall into a restless sleep until she heard him come upstairs and go into his room.

The household fell into a new routine. Zack was gone most of the day every day. Sometimes Camille caught a brief glimpse of him in the mornings before he rushed out. Other days it wasn't until dinnertime that she saw her husband. Though they tried to keep up a happy facade for Rayburn, she wondered if the older man was fooled.

It was puzzling to her that Zack had made a romantic overture to her. He obviously hated her. Why had he bothered to accost her in the bathroom? She had only to look at Rayburn's hopeful face to find her answer. He wanted an heir for Bridal Wreath. Was Zack's motivation in wanting to make love to her to provide his father with that longed for grandchild? Sadly, she reasoned that it must be.

She spent most of her time with Rayburn. They worked with his plants, took slow walking tours of the lower floor of the house while she pointed out the final stages of decorating, and even went for brief strolls around the terrace in the backyard when his strength and the weather permitted it.

The weather didn't allow many of those days. It had been a very wet and dreary month. It rained nearly every day, and, when it wasn't raining, the clouds hung heavy and threatening over the landscape. Camille's depression seemed intensified by the outside gloom and the cold rain that came down in torrents. Would there be no end to this unhappy situation?

To her further humiliation, Zack continued to go out nearly every evening. He rarely left just after dinner, but most usually he waited until Rayburn had retired for the night before leaving. There was no doubt in Camille's mind where these nightly sojourns led him. He went straight to Erica Hazelett's arms.

Vainly she tried to keep her hopelessness and listlessness out of her eyes, but she failed to do so. Her mirror told her that she looked pale and haggard. Her eyes were often puffy and red from crying and lack of sleep.

It was on one of those rainy, cold, dismal days

that she and Rayburn were sitting in his den looking through a picture album that he had asked her
to help him organize. She looked at photographs of
Zack as an infant, a young boy, and a student. He
grinned back at her wearing basketball shorts, track
shorts, baseball uniforms, and even from behind a
football helmet. Was there nothing he didn't excel
in? There were prom night pictures with a girl
swathed in pink organza clinging to his arm. Was
this the girl that he had loved? The one who had
hurt him so deeply? The one he was trying to forget
in Snow Bird? Had they dated for years, and then
as an adult had she decided to marry someone else?

There was a serious Zack in a cap and gown at
his high school graduation, and a beaming college
graduate with a tight grip around his father's shoulders. Camille's heart swelled with pride and pain.
This was a part of Zack's life she could never share
with him. Now it seemed as if she'd share none of it.

Before she could control them, tears spilled
down her cheeks and fell into the trembling hands
covering her face.

"Now, my dear, please don't get upset. I can't
stand to see you this way." Rayburn offered her a
snowy handkerchief that she used to stem the flow
of tears though their source refused to check them
completely.

"I . . . I'm sorry, Rayburn," she sputtered. ""I
don't want to upset you. I'm so ashamed."

He enfolded her in his arms and stroked her

shoulders. "There has never been anything for you to be ashamed of, Camille." He spoke with parental concern. "When I first saw you in Atlanta, I had a flickering hope in the back of my mind that you and Zachary might find each other attractive. You reminded me of my Alice. Oh, not physically. But you had a radiance about you that she had had. It's a rare thing to see such exhuberance for living in a woman any more. It seems as though women have forgotten to be feminine, glad in their womanhood. Careers are fine. I'm no chauvinist. But I still like to see a woman who glories in the fact that she is just that. A woman. I'm old-fashioned, I realize." He paused reflectively for a moment as if trying to regain his train of thought after his digression.

"That first afternoon that you were here, I could feel the currents flashing between you and Zachary. Of course, then, I didn't know about what had happened in Utah almost two years before. Funny how coincidences happen, isn't it? That morning in the hospital when I awoke to the sound of you two scuffling on that ridiculous rollaway bed, I was thrilled. Please don't be embarrassed," he said kindly as he reached out to pat her hand. He had noticed her deep blush. "It's perfectly natural that you should delight in each other's bodies. Alice and I . . . well, anyway, it took a lot of restraint to keep from shouting my joy that you two were caught in an affectionate clench. By that time, I had come to love you, too, Camille. I couldn't have chosen a woman I'd rather have for a daughter, and wife for my son." He looked deeply into her tear-flooded eyes and stroked her cheek softly. "Then imagine my dismay when I heard the conversation that was to follow. Had I not been sick and weak, my son would probably have been on the receiving end of a beating. I was furious with him for making you carry such guilt and remorse. And the way he talked to you was shameful. I was glad his mother wasn't around to hear it. That's when I conceived the plan to surprise you with a wedding."

Camille hung her head shamefacedly. "You did it then only in compensation for Zack's behavior in Utah?"

"No, my dear. I did it because I thought—and still think—that you and Zachary love each other and just won't admit it. If you had been a hussy or a schemer or someone otherwise undesirable, I would have forgotten the incident then and there. If I hadn't thought a great love and beautiful, intelligent children could come out of this alliance, I would never have taken such drastic measures to bring you together."

"I know your motives were pure, Rayburn." Camille couldn't meet his knowing eyes. She looked down at her lap, over his head, around the room, trying to escape the intelligent blue eyes, hooded by bushy white eyebrows that victimized whomever they gazed upon. "It's just that . . . Zack and I . . . It's just not going to work out. I wish for your sake that it could. I honestly do, but . . ." her voice trailed off. *But your son doesn't love me,* she silently added. *He loves someone else.*

"It has grieved me to see the two of you so unhappy, Camille. I hoped that if I forced you into marriage you would recognize the love I still insist you have for each other, but I'm a reasonable man, and I can't hold you to a union that makes you and Zachary both so abysmally miserable. I'm going to miss you, Camille, when you go, as I know you will. You're too honest to go on forever living a lie. And please remember that you always have a home here at Bridal Wreath."

"Thank you, Rayburn," she said around her constricted throat. She leaned over and kissed his forehead. "You can rest now, and don't worry about any of this. You couldn't have known that Zack and I have problems that can't be resolved."

Before she left the room, Rayburn halted her. "Camille, the day after tomorrow is Thanksgiving. Would you stay until then? Indulge an old man one more time. I want us to be a family on that day."

"Of course I will," she promised. Then she added, almost as an afterthought, "You'll always be my family."

Twelve

*L*ike women all over America, Camille and Dearly spent most of the next day in the kitchen preparing food for the Thanksgiving meal. Camille did the odd jobs like chopping fruits and nuts, washing vegetables and greens for salads, and measuring condiments for Dearly, who mixed them together with astounding alacrity, creating the most delicious-looking and aromatic dishes Camille's taste buds had ever anticipated.

"I won't interfere if you don't want me to, but I've been told even by my mother that I make a pretty good pecan pie," Camille teased the cook.

"Be my guest, Camille. And I happen to know that pecan is Zack's favorite." She rolled her dark eyes and threw Camille a goading look.

"Well, I hope that everyone will enjoy it," Camille remarked noncommittally.

Later in the afternoon she was tiredly going up the stairs when Zack's voice stopped her.

"Camille." She turned toward him in surprise. He had not initiated a conversation with her for the past week, and she couldn't imagine what he wanted with her now. He mounted a few of the steps until he stood just below her. When he reached his hand up toward her face, she flinched and drew back quickly. The lines around his mouth hardened and the planes of his jaw went rigid.

"I was only going to brush away a spot of flour on your cheek," he said very low. "Actually it looks quite charming." He stared at her pensively for a few moments before he continued. "I know you and Dearly have been working all day in the kitchen, and she's tired. Dad suggested that we go out to dinner and give her the night off. I'm going to fix him something before we leave. Is that all right with you? We haven't been to Under-the-Hill yet, so I thought we'd go there and eat catfish."

It didn't mater to him that she was tired, too. *He* hadn't wanted to take her out to dinner. Rayburn had suggested it. She had a momentary flair of resentment and started to tell him "no, thank you," but he looked so handsome standing on the stair below her, staring up at her with those azure eyes that never failed to stir her. She was going to leave soon, and this might be one of the few times that she and Zack would be alone together. Her decision was made. "Yes, that sounds nice," she said calmly, though her heart was racing. She wasn't going to let him see how the prospect of being alone with him for an evening affected her.

"It's okay to go casual. Where we're going, jeans are fine. Besides, the weather isn't conducive to dressing up."

She glanced over his shoulder to the windows beside the front door and saw that the rain hadn't abated.

"Fine. What time?"

"How long does it take to wash the flour off your face?" She was too flustered to answer right away, and, when he saw her confusion, he reached up and took possession of one of her hands. The touch of his fingers seared her skin, and she felt the tingle all the way up her arm. "Hey, I was only joking! Let's say seven o'clock and make it an early evening. Okay?"

He no doubt had a late date with Erica. "Okay," she replied dispiritedly, and, reluctantly withdrawing her hand from his, retreated upstairs.

Natchez-Under-the-Hill was rich in history. At one time the settlement under the bluffs overlooking the Mississippi River had boasted five streets. It had been the site of numerous bawdy houses, taverns, gambling establishments, and any number of less than circumspect businesses. As if in judgment for all the iniquitous deeds that happened in this unsavory part of the city, God used the river to eat away at the banks and reduced Natchez-Under-the-Hill to only one street and a smattering of buildings. Most of these antique structures had been converted into fashionable boutiques, drinking establishments, and antique stores. The area was a main tourist attraction.

Zack explained all of this as he negotiated his Lincoln down Silver Street, which was the only road that led down the steep incline to Under-the-Hill. Camille was nervous at the thought of coming up this same way when they planned to leave. The road was already treacherously slick with heavy rainfall and mud that had washed from the bluffs.

"They even used Under-the-Hill for Civil War Atlanta one time when they filmed a movie here. They put stacks of old tires behind some of the vacant buildings and lit them to represent General Sherman's burning of your city. They had covered the pavement with dirt so it would look authentic and brought in about forty horse-drawn vehicles. It was quite a show and very effective. The movie companies use our antebellum houses frequently for sets, but that was the first time I remember them using Under-the-Hill in a film."

He maneuvered the car into one of the few parking spaces allotted along the sidewalk. It lined the front of the buildings facing the river. "If it weren't raining, we'd have parked at the top of the bluff and walked down. The parking situation down here leaves a lot to be desired," Zack complained before stepping out of the car and dashing around to her door, holding an umbrella over his head.

They managed to dodge puddles and negotiate the uneven sidewalk till they reached the entrance of the restaurant. The Cock of the Walk restaurant lived up to its reputation. The delicious fried catfish accompanied by a variety of side dishes and the warm friendly ambience of the dining room relaxed Camille, and she enjoyed the meal with Zack. He, too, seemed relaxed and eager to talk, to share. Their conversation centered mainly around the plantation and particularly the horse-breeding enterprise. Zack became excited over the prospects of his new undertaking, and Camille was able for a few minutes to forget that she wouldn't be here to see the success she was sure he would achieve.

Her eyes were swimming with tears as she looked at her husband over the candlelit table. Her voice was constricted, and she averted her head so that he might not see how highly strung her emotions were as she mumbled, "I'm sure you'll realize much success from it, Zack."

"Success?" His voice was soft but harsh. "Yes, I guess monetary gain is one measure of success, but, in the important areas of my life, I have failed miserably."

Camille risked a glance at him, but he wasn't looking at her. He was studying the wall behind her. His words wounded her deeply. No, he didn't have everything he wanted, did he? He wasn't living with the woman he truly loved. He was stuck with a wife whom he barely tolerated. How Zack must resent her presence in his life! Camille longed to reach out and take the long, strong hand that lay on the table, press it to her cheek, and assure him that she would no longer be an unwelcome element in his life. She would leave the day after Thanksgiving. That would fulfill her promise to Rayburn and at the same time hasten their inevitable separation. She would slip quietly out of his life—as quietly as she had slipped into it two years ago at Snow Bird. This time when she left him, he would feel only relief and not the bitterness that he had before. This time his male ego would be intact, and he would have Erica's willing arms to find solace in.

"Are you finished?" Zack's question interrupted her reverie.

"Yes," she answered shakily. He came around to her chair and held it for her. When he had settled the bill and they were standing at the front door, he held her coat for her. She felt the strong hands rest briefly on her shoulders before he withdrew them. How she longed to lean against his strength! If he would hold her once more, create a memory to carry her through a lifetime of loneliness, maybe leaving wouldn't be so painful. But wouldn't such an embrace only make it harder to leave him?

It was still raining hard when they emerged from the coziness of the restaurant. Zack opened the umbrella and held it over them as they started making their way back to the parked car. The river was almost invisible through the sheets of rain even this close. The rain obscured nearly everything, making the night black, ominous.

They walked past one of the taverns, and as Camille looked through the large plate-glass windows, she noticed that it was almost deserted. There were no more than a dozen people seeking recreation by playing electronic games or backgammon and sipping drinks at small tables lit by soft lamps. Faint strains of music from a jukebox could be heard through the old brick walls, and Camille recognized a popular ballad. Later, for years afterward, whenever she heard that song, she would tremble in recollection of what happened seconds later.

It was the strange noise that first caught her attention. It was a combination of crunching and sucking sounds that was discordant, out of sync, awesome. Of one accord, she and Zack paused on the sidewalk listening to that puzzling, horrendous racket.

Looking through the window of the tavern she stood mesmerized as she saw the back wall of the building seem to move forward several inches before it began to crumble. The electric clock with an animated advertisement for a brand of beer on its face flew off the wall and shattered on the floor. Old movie posters hung in decorative frames swung precariously on their hooks before falling to the floor and being covered by falling bricks and mortar.

What was it? What was happening? Tornado? No, there was no wind. Earthquake? No, the ground wasn't vibrating through Camille was certain that the fearful rumble-crash sound she heard was much like the sounds of one.

The few people in the bar stopped their easy chatter, their game-playing, their drinking, and stared as she did at the collapsing wall. Then fright spurred them into action. En masse they ran for the door, terror written on their faces, screams coming from the throats of even the brawniest men.

"God! It's a mud slide!" shouted Zack into her ear and began tugging on her elbow in an effort to snap her out of her hypnotized state. She had matched his running steps for only a few feet before the entire front of the building came crashing onto the sidewalk in front of them. Lumber, bricks, and glass were forced shatteringly together, propelled forward by the oozing, sucking mud. As one portion of the building fell, relinquishing its support, another section began to give way in a domino reaction under the weight of the mud that continued to slide down from the bluffs above. The ones who had been trapped in the building fought their way through broken windows, doors, and walls trying to gain freedom from the mud, which would spell instant suffocation for a victim if he weren't killed by falling debris. They were in a panic bred of self-preservation.

Camille saw one last support beam of the building crumble under the incredible weight that ever increased. Zack! was her only thought. With strength garnered from an extra spurt of adrenaline, she extricated her elbow from his grasp and shoved him away from her and off the sidewalk. Her unexpected and amazingly strong shove unbalanced him. He slipped on the cracked, uneven concrete. Camille saw him fall off the sidewalk and roll out into the street to relative safety a few yards away. The umbrella was hopelessly broken as he fell on it. It lay discarded in the muddy street.

Zack raised his head and shook the rain out of his eyes. With a detached part of her mind, Camille noted that his hair was plastered to his head from the rain. His clothes were covered with mud.

"I love you!" she screamed above the cacophony.

His eyes widened in a dawning of understanding then went blank with horror. She heard him shout her name before a blinding pain struck the back of her head. She fought the darkness descending over her consciousness; she felt her knees buckling and saw the sidewalk rushing up to meet her. *I'm going to die,* she thought calmly. Her last conscious thought was a prayer of thanksgiving that Zack was safe.

She could hear the rain. She could hear muffled

voices. She smelled an acrid antiseptic lotion. She could feel that her clothes were damp and clinging.

She wasn't dead.

She tried to open her eyes, but the slit of light that she allowed through her lids burst upon her brain like a searchlight, and she squeezed her eyes shut against it.

Someone raised her arm, and she started in reaction.

"Hey, don't you even know who your friends are? I'm only taking your blood pressure, Camille."

"Dr. . . ." It was a croak. She cleared her throat and tried again. "Dr. Daniels, is that you?"

"None other. What other dumb bastard would come out on a night like this?"

"Where? . . . Zack? . . . What happened?"

"One question at a time please." She was grateful for his strong reassuring hands on her arms. His voice was as brusque as always, but it was kind and familiar. "You're in an ambulance. Do you remember the mud slide?" At her nod, he continued, "Well, you got quite a knock on the noggin from a falling brick, but you'll be okay. You don't have a concussion, just a bitch of a headache."

She smiled in spite of the pain and tried once again to open her eyes. This time she went about it more carefully and had more success. The doctor's caricature of a face came into view, blurred and double-imaged at first, but then clearer as she blinked and opened her eyes wider.

"Zack?"

He patted her arm. "No one was killed. A few people were injured, but everyone was lucky to come out alive. It's one hell of a mess out there, but the fire department is working on it. Seems with the continuous rain we've had, the bluffs became saturated and couldn't hold any more. A big chunk of earth broke off and started an avalanche of mud."

Thank God no one had died! But Zack . . . ?

"I'm going to give you a shot now, and you won't remember much after this. It'll knock you on your can. Here it comes." She felt the needle prick her upper arm. "I don't think you need to go to the hospital, but if you have more than a dull headache tomorrow, call me."

Why wouldn't he tell her anything about Zack? Was he seriously injured? She had seen him safe in the street. She remembered that now. But what if he had been injured after she had been struck down? Or killed! No, Dr. Daniels had said no one had been killed. But would he tell her the truth if it were Zack? Was he dead? He couldn't be dead before she had a chance to tell him she loved him! Zack!

Her mind was getting fuzzy, and her tongue felt thick and furry. The doctor's injection was already affecting her. Her eyes were closing involuntarily, and her head was throbbing.

"Zack? Zack? Where is Zack? He's dead; I

know it. Is he dead?" Her voice was shrill in the confines of the ambulance.

"Dead! Hell no, he's not dead. He's a real pain in the ass! He's acting just about as hysterical and crazy as you're working yourself up to be. God, I pity the doctor who delivers your babies." He turned to an ambulance attendant who had been giving oxygen to a man on another stretcher. "Go get her husband, will you? You can't miss him. He's the one with the maniacal eyes."

Zack shoved the paramedic out of the way as he rushed through the door of the ambulance. He looked deranged. He could have passed for a fugitive from Bedlam.

He knelt beside the stretcher and searched Camille's face for signs of injury. She smiled at him tremulously and wanted to speak, but her tongue couldn't quite get the message to her befuddled brain. She longed to reach up and push back the curls lying limply on his forehead, to smooth the worry lines etched there, but her arms were too heavy, and she couldn't lift them.

Zack kissed her tenderly on the forehead and then on her closed eyelids. "You said you love me. I heard you, Camille. You love me." Her surprise knew no limits when he buried his face against her stomach and clutched her to him. "God, Camille, I thought I'd lost you again."

What did he mean? When had he lost her before? She must already be unconscious and dreaming this. But she was sure she could feel his ragged breathing and a strange moisture coming from his eyes. His hands were moving over her arms, weren't they? Weren't his fingers gently tracing the planes of her face?

His words echoed through her brain. God, Camille, I thought I'd lost you again. God, Camille, I thought I'd lost you . . . God, Camille, I thought . . .

She was having that wonderful dream again about Snow Bird. She didn't want to wake up and have to leave the dream. She wanted to stay in it with Zack. She never wanted to leave him again. Please, God, let the dream last this time. It was so good.

She woke up, but the dream continued. There was the fireplace across the room. Heavy drapes were pulled closed over the wide windows making the room dim. She and Zack were lying naked in the vast bed, her body curled against the long, hard curve of his. One possessive arm was flung across her hip. They were sharing the same pillow. She could feel his sweet breath fanning the back of her neck.

This wasn't a dream! This wasn't the room in Snow Bird! This was Zack's room at Bridal Wreath, and they lived here together as husband and wife. Her contented, grateful sigh must have awakened him, for he stirred behind her.

She rolled over slightly and looked up at him as he leaned over her and studied her closely for indications of pain. "My darling," he whispered, "how do you feel?" His lips barely touched hers in a soft kiss.

Had he called her "darling"? Was he kissing her tenderly? Maybe this *was* a dream. If so, she wished it would go on forever. She didn't want to wake up. With fear that the figment would vanish, she said softly, "I'm wonderful, Zack. I'm here with you, and we're both alive, and I'm wonderful."

"Camille," he choked. "I love you so much." He buried his face in the hollow of her throat and covered it with impassioned kisses. "My love, my sweet love—"

His lips found hers. His kiss was tender and conveyed a meaning far too puissant for mere words. Her mouth responded in kind, opening under his and matching his ardor. When at last he drew away, he stroked back strands of unruly dark hair and curled a stray lock around his fingers. "This is how it should have been with us the next morning in Utah. I should have told you that night how much I loved you before we . . . I was afraid you wouldn't believe me. A girl as beautiful as you must have heard every clever line in the book, I thought. Would you have believed me if I had started expounding on my love for you?"

She smiled and confidently explored his chest

with her fingertips. "Probably not. I thought you were very sophisticated."

"Is that a tactful way of saying you thought I was old? I must have seemed ancient to you! Do I still?" His breath was coming in short gasps as she continued to touch him intimately.

"Zack! Of course not! Your age intimidated me, though. I was frightened of you. That's why I couldn't tell you that I was falling in love with you. I was afraid you'd laugh at me. I was sure you'd look upon me as a one-night stand. I didn't dare risk your ridicule, so I left."

"You mean that's the reason you ran out on me?! Oh, Camille, how stupid and proud we've been. I thought I repelled you in some way. How much precious time we've wasted!" He kissed her again, wanting to make up for all that lost time. His mouth went to her ear, and his tongue traced its delicate lines as he whispered, "Then you *do* love me, Camille?"

His caresses were causing a tickling sensation in her throat and she could barely articulate her answer. "Yes, Zack, I love you. I have ever since the first time I saw you."

Stroking fingers smoothed the skin from her collar bone to her navel. It was a distracting movement, but she tried to concentrate on what he was saying. "I was like a man possessed when I woke up that morning and found you gone. Pride kept me from going to your friends and asking how to reach you. You had told me you went to school in Richmond, but never mentioned being from Atlanta. I called every Jameson in Richmond and none of them had a daughter, sister, or second cousin named Camille. I was on the wrong track all that time. When I came home, I was unbearable to live with. No one dared cross me for fear of my temper. My moods were volatile—"

"You mean *I* was the one!" she exclaimed. "I was the woman you couldn't get over?" When she saw his puzzled expression, she explained about Dearly's telling her that he had gone through a "black period" over a woman. "I thought you'd gone to Utah to get over your beautiful, lost love and used me to restore your self-image."

"You are the only woman I've ever loved, Camille. And you are definitely beautiful." He was nibbling her shoulders while his hands stroked her hips and thighs.

"Erica—?" She had to know everything. There would be no more secrets or ghosts between them.

His hands stilled, and he raised his head. He looked away from her for a moment then met her eyes steadily. "I've slept with her, Camille, in desperation, but I've never loved her."

"But after our wedding, in the restaurant, I heard you tell her that our marriage made no difference in how you felt about her."

He chuckled softly. "I told her the truth. My marriage to you didn't alter my feelings for her. I

don't like her and never did. She is the most selfish, conniving, manipulative woman I've ever
known. Each time I was with her, I came away
sick with myself. Instead of appeasing my longing
for you, I only missed your sweetness and innocence more."

"And these nights that you've been going out—"

He laughed. "Jealous, were you?" He kissed her
nose. "Well, you were supposed to be. Actually, I
spent most of those long, cold nights in the horse
barn at the plantation. A couple of nights, I went
fishing, and I *hate* to fish. A few nights, I just
parked the car near the river and watched the
barges go by until it was late enough to come
home. I made plenty of noise so you couldn't fail
to note the lateness of the hour."

"I never even noticed you were gone," she said,
suppressing a feigned yawn.

"Like hell, you didn't," he growled and covered
her mouth with a possessive kiss. When they were
breathless, he pulled away to look down on her
adoringly. "Camille, I love you, but I have a confession to make." His eyes lit up with a mischievous gleam that she had come to know well. This
confession was not going to be a serious one. "I
like the dining room."

She pretended indignation, but reached out to
tickle his ribs. "Oh, Zack! You're exasperating."
She stared up at him, loving him. "You have your
nerve bringing me to your bed this way when I

wasn't able to defend myself! And on Thanksgiving morning, too."

His smile was wicked. "Well, this just gives me that much more to be thankful for."

"Zack, don't be irreverent."

"Besides," he continued, ignoring her. "I don't think you really mind, do you?" He was lazily caressing her breasts, watching with fascination as the nipples became aroused under his fingers.

For an answer, she tangled her fingers in his hair and forced his head down to hers. "Make love to me," she whispered.

"Are you sure you don't have a headache?" He was serious, but they both laughed when they simultaneously caught the double entendre.

"If I do," she answered, "I'll take an aspirin. But later . . . much later."

5